Down at the Dock

Down at the Dock

More Stories of the Good Life in the Northwoods

Mike Lein

Jackpine Writers' Bloc, Inc.
Menahga, Minnesota 56464

Some of the chapters in this book have appeared in edited forms in other publications as noted below.

Kayak Angler: "Escape from Stumpfire Island."

Lake Country Journal Magazine: "Aunt Mickey's Rhubarb," "Things You Don't Want to Hear at Deer Camp," and excerpts from "A Walk in the Woods—Foraying with the Paul Bunyan Mushroom Club."

Minnesota Conservation Volunteer: "Black Powder in the Bunyan," "Cabin Talk."

Star Tribune: excerpts from "Expert Advice."

Talking Stick books: "The Perfect Crime," "A River Runs Through It."

All illustrations and cover artwork contributed by Erik Espeland.

Acknowledgments

Writing the stories that make up *Down at the Dock* was the easy part of this book—my second. The harder part was pulling them together and editing the draft so that it made sense and looked good. For that I need to acknowledge the assistance of the publisher— the Jackpine Writers' Bloc, Inc., of Menahga, Minnesota. Sharon Harris and Tarah L. Wolff get credit for the main editing and formatting. Other members tolerated my stories at meetings, offered suggestions and constructive critiques that added depth and action to the stories. And then there's Jerry Mevissen, Jackpine Writers' Bloc member, writer, mentor, and Marketing Manager extraordinaire. Thanks!

Credit for the cover art and book illustrations goes to Erik Espeland of Field Hands. I put him on a deadline with the mandate to make the art for this book bigger and better than our first collaboration— *Firewood Happens*. He came through despite a new addition to his family.

Several of the stories in *Down at the Dock* were previously published in magazines and anthologies. There's nothing like an acceptance notice and a check showing up in the mailbox to keep a guy interested in writing. Acceptance of articles by the editors of *The Minnesota Conservation Volunteer*, *The Lake Country Journal Magazine*, *Kayak Angler*, and *The Talking Stick* provided instant gratification and kept me writing.

Finally, thanks to all the friends, family, and other acquaintances that played roles in these stories and in the actual construction of our cabin. If I didn't have interesting people in my life, I wouldn't have a cabin or adventures to write about.

Table of Contents

Down at the Dock

More Stories of the Good Life in the Northwoods

Expert Advice

In 1992, Marcie and I made a big decision. After watching Lake Country land and cabin prices escalate for years, now was the time to take the plunge and find our own place. The search for the perfect spot was time-consuming and involved bushwhacking through "heavily wooded lots" to survey building sites, wading barefoot into weedy undeveloped lakeshore, dealing with thousands of blood-sucking bugs, and one massive case of poison ivy. The end of the search was five acres of woods on a small lake that met most of our criteria—including a no down payment contract for deed purchase arrangement.

We spent the first years camping in the warmer months, clearing brush, battling bugs, and having all kinds of fun with our two sons, dogs, and friends. It didn't take us long to want more—a cabin where we could hunt, cross-country ski, ice fish, and have fun all year long.

Given the realities of our financial situation and jobs, it would have to be a small, simple cabin, one that we could build ourselves and afford to maintain. I spent many a night drawing up cabin plans and figuring construction budgets, trying to find the right mix of size and cost. The basement for the 16x20-foot cabin was dug in August of 1998. We then proceeded to build the cabin the old fashioned way—do-it-yourself labor from a host of talented and not-so-talented family and friends. Like any real cabin, it has a woodstove for heat and an outhouse. We don't need to keep it heated or worry about pipes and sewer systems freezing in the winter. It should be finished sometime this century.

Visitors often ask how we chose our location, why the cabin is so small, and who picked the materials. I'm here to answer those questions. Here's a list of hits and misses, pro and cons.

Location. We picked five acres on a lake classified by the State of Minnesota as a "Natural Environment Lake." With that classification comes requirements for larger lots and building setbacks, more shoreline, and less disturbance of the shoreline. We don't regret that for a moment. That's what we wanted—a natural setting. Not a suburban housing neighborhood. It would be nice if we had less elevation from the lake and maybe a walleye or two swimming in it.

Size. I agonized over the size of the cabin while drawing the plans. I needed to keep expenses down and the size manageable given that I would be doing most of the work, crawling around on ladders alone in the woods, humping plywood sheets and shingle bundles via manpower, using a generator for construction tool power. Things like that. I compromised on a split-foyer design that limited the height I'd be working at, the cost of the materials, and the sheer scope of the project. In hindsight, it would have been nice to add another four feet or so. On the other hand, the compact well-insulated cabin heats up fast when arriving in the dead of a cold winter night. I know other owners who have trouble getting their larger cabins warm for a winter weekend trip.

Design. My design included a walk-out, half-story basement on the lake side. This would be the main living area with a basic kitchen, woodstove, dining table, couch, and comfy chairs. The second floor, with five-foot side walls and a vaulted ceiling, would be the sleeping area with a possible loft added later in construction. I didn't want the lower floor to feel like a basement since three of the walls would be buried four feet into the hillside. A full eight-foot ceiling and two windows on each side were added to try and keep it open and spacious and not feel like an enclosed basement.

This turned out to be the biggest design flaw, if you want to call it that. The lower level still felt like a "basement" once it was capped and I started working on the second floor. The view was better from above and with the vaulted ceiling provided a larger open-air atmosphere. I changed plans in mid-construction and added larger windows on the upper floor. It was obvious this was where we would want to spend time. Looking out the windows, downhill through the shoreline trees, gives it a treehouse-like feeling. Or, as other folks have stated, like living in a big deer stand.

Foundation. Having spent some time working in the cement construction trade during college summers, I had few qualms about tackling the foundation. And I wanted it to be the brick outhouse of foundations. We poured massive footings and built up using cement poured into insulated foam building blocks. Think building a cabin with huge toy interlocking blocks. I'd do it again and probably will for the next addition. The foam blocks were easy to assemble and provided instant insulation without another step. I did hire an employee of the foam block manufacturer to oversee and assist on construction day. He and the basement excavator ended up being the only non-friend/relative paid help that have worked on the cabin to date.

Construction Labor. I did much of the construction by myself. Pounding nails while listening to gunshots from other guys grouse- and duck-hunting in the surrounding State Forest. Installing windows while neighbors ice fished out on the lake. Digging the outhouse hole by hand while mosquitoes and deer flies bit and chewed my flesh. My past construction experience got me through most projects. Others required assistance—like the physical labor for pouring cement, the electrical knowledge for wiring, and crafting the joints in the siding. I leaned heavily on friends and relatives for these. The only downfall of this cheap source of labor (besides all the free beer) was the length of time it took to accomplish major projects one weekend at a time. A construction crew of professionals would have been much faster.

Electricity. One of the major decisions we faced was power. Live off the grid with a generator, solar and/or other alternatives? Or hook into the conventional power-line 900 feet away on the county road? The main structure was built with hand tools and electricity from a small portable generator. Propane and kerosene lights and heaters gave us light and warmth after dark. But when I found out the local electrical co-op was willing to run a line to the site for no cost, the main power decision was easy. Especially when considering the close family ties to an Electrical Engineer. I followed, brother Steve led.

His handiwork passed the electrical inspection on the second attempt. This was the right decision for us given the minimal cost of the labor and materials.

Siding. I never seriously considered building an actual log cabin. I love the look but the upfront expense and the potential problems like settling and shrinkage and lack of actual construction experience scared me off. We opted for conventional 2x6 construction covered with locally milled log siding. It's not maintenance free. A coat of oil-based semi-transparent stain needs to be added to the south side every three years. That's the price you pay for the Up North look. Application of the siding was also tougher than expected. My limited tools and experience just couldn't make the mitered joints look good. I called in my good friend and building contractor, Kim. He did it right and he worked for beer.

Interior. Once the outside was under control, we moved indoors. Locally produced random-length aspen tongue-and-groove was an easy selection here. By now we had electricity and an air nailer. This was a great husband/wife project with Marcie selecting and fetching the boards while I nailed them down. A couple of coats of clear finish later and the light color and consistent pattern of the aspen combines with the vaulted ceiling for an open airy look. We'll add more in the lower level—when we get around to it.

Woodstove. With five acres of heavily wooded land right on the edge of thousands of acres of forest —think potential firewood—a woodstove was an easy decision to make. I know insurance agents hate them and wood can be dirty, messy, and labor-intensive to obtain. But a cabin isn't a cabin without a woodstove— at least in my opinion. We researched stoves, bought a well-built EPA-certified one, and installed the best triple-lined stainless steel chimney available. We may use electric space heaters for back-up heat and to assist in the initial warm-up on cold winter arrivals. The woodstove keeps on burning home-grown firewood, churning out heat with no worries of power outages. The lower level entry door limits the mess in the main living area.

Deck. I struggled with building front steps that were functional and looked good. The front steps ended up being a 10x12-foot deck. Problem solved. It is the fair weather seating area of choice for almost six months of the year. It doesn't have a view of the lake but it does get you up off the ground away from the bugs and provides a grand view of the bird feeders and ongoing wildlife activity. An upgrade to a screened porch is definitely in the plans.

Outhouse. When it comes to the need for facilities, I have an advantage over many people. The first ten or eleven years of my life were spent living on farms without indoor bathrooms. So a trip to the outhouse is a nostalgic moment for me. Marcie is willing to suffer along—at least for now. The next addition will include a well, sewer system, and indoor facilities. It just wasn't in the financial picture for this phase and we don't have to worry about pipes freezing or "closing" the cabin. So if you don't like using an outhouse, keep your visits to our place short —or invite us to your place.

The interior of the cabin is still a work in progress. The lower level is largely unfinished and some details like flooring are missing in the upper level. Regarding that, I have to admit I'm getting used to the look and ease of maintenance provided by area rugs over plywood. We keep picking away, adding little details like a granite shelf and wrought iron vent panels with outdoorsy designs. Those will keep us busy while planning the next addition. When will that be? I don't really know. This project has only taken twenty years. Why be in a hurry when you have a cabin to enjoy?

Smartphone Follies

Youngest son Steve and I head down to the dock with the dogs on a sunny summer day. Murri, the fluffy little terrier/poodle combo, leads the way, having been acclimated to lake life by the old Labrador and now seeming to believe she is a Labrador. We follow the switchback trail to the steps that ease the way down the last twenty feet to the dock. It's time for a refreshing swim and a little dock time after a hard day of fishing, lawn mowing, and other typical cabin duties.

I set down the dock bag loaded with a couple of cold adult beverages, towels, and camera and stop to admire the view. Steve strips off his T-shirt and eggs the dogs on—"Come on, girls. Let's hit the lake!"

He and Kal sprint down the dock and do a synchronized geysering cannonball into the cool water of Crooked Lake. Murri hits the water a moment behind them with a far lesser splash and paddles circles around Steve. Kal effortlessly cruises through the lily pads looking for something, anything, to retrieve.

I wait until they are clear and prepare for my own run down the dock, anticipating the bracing shock of the initial splash down. Something feels wrong. I stop short, teetering at the edge.

"Hey, what's wrong—you coming in or not?" Steve challenges me.

I silently reach into the pocket of my swimsuit, remove the expensive, non-waterproof, non-protected-by-a-replacement-plan smartphone and hold it up.

"Hah!" he laughs. "You almost ruined another one!"

Cellphones, especially smartphones, are a controversial issue at cabins. Use or don't use, unplug or plug in, keep in touch or drop off the grid. Everyone has a different philosophy. Some cabin owners have rules requiring them to be turned over and locked away. I can heartily agree with the "forget about them" philosophy. Who wants to be reminded of work here, surrounded by friends and nature? Why not drop out of the rat race for a few days and forget what's happening out there beyond the beach?

But life is complicated these days. I still need to stay in touch with people who write me checks, partially so I can afford the cabin. Those folks are a lot happier when they can get in touch with me if stuff happens. It's also true that living in the woods has gotten more convenient and safe. Stuck in the snow trying to get to some secret lake for ice fishing? Outboard motor broke down out on the lake? I can just call neighbor Marv with the smartphone. He's retired and always seems to have time to help the needy.

It's also handy down on the dock. Our cabin has "elevation" as they say in the real estate business. If I wander down to the dock and forget something important, like two beverages when I only brought one, I can always call uphill to Marcie and convince her that she needs to come down and enjoy the lake on such a beautiful day. And bring a few more beverages while she's at it.

Most smartphones aren't waterproof and don't float. No need to experiment with this yourself. I've already done that for you. One fell off the dock and

🐕

was easily retrieved. It didn't work even after I tried Internet-recommended cures such as drying out in a bag of rice. The one I dropped down the ice fishing hole on Red Lake sank like a rock and was not recovered.

I took some grief from Marcie (and a few other people) for that one. After all, it was only a week old and I had been too cheap to buy the replacement warranty. But here's another lesson: never make fun of the person who loses or ruins their phone in the lake. You might be next. The spring after my ice fishing mishap, Marcie bent over the side of the boat to free her crappie jig from an underwater snag. HER non-replacement-plan, non-waterproof, sinking cellphone fell out of her life jacket pocket. Nope, it didn't land in the boat. It's now remotely possible that the walleyes in Red Lake can take advantage of our Friends and Family Plan with my phone and have the crappies in Crooked Lake answer on Marcie's phone. I'll be watching the bills just in case.

I've learned a few lessons at least. Since it's unrealistic for me to not carry the dang thing around and, since history tends to repeat itself, bad stuff is going to happen. So I'm budgeting for the replacement plan on my next phone. And while I'm at it, I am going to shop for a swimsuit without pockets.

My Private Lake

The morning sun was only a faint glow in the northeast when I awoke to the gurgle of the automatic coffee pot. I stayed in bed as the coffee brewed, listening to the awakening world through the open windows of the cabin. Most of yesterday had been a constant drizzling rain. Now the early birds were making up for lost time at 5 a.m. Woodpeckers were screeching and drumming on hollow trees. Finches and hummingbirds were cheeping and buzzing at feeders. Loudest and most persistent of all were the robins, belting out their rhythmic calls from the surrounding woods.

I forced myself out of the warm bed, pulled on a few clothes, and checked the weather while letting Kaliber out for her morning stroll. Calm and foggy with a hint of a fine mist, just the kind of day I was hoping for. I fought off the grogginess of a too-short night, filled the Thermos with fresh coffee, and grabbed a couple of granola bars. The truck was ready and waiting with the small red Lund fishing boat hitched behind. Just the kind of rig for where we were headed on this early June morn.

Summer is a busy time in northern Minnesota. Check popular lakes any weekend after Memorial Day and there will be a frenzied madness of fishermen, pleasure boaters, skiers, and Jet Skiers competing for the same water. But even here in Vacation Land, you can find solitude if you are willing to get up early on a Tuesday morning, brave less than ideal weather, and go exploring.

To reach the lake I had in mind meant being

willing to get the truck and boat dirty. I drove ten miles into the forest, winding down gravel minimum maintenance roads, trying to dodge rocks and a thousand potholes filled with muddy water. Kal rode shotgun whining with excitement. The small parking area of the lake access wasn't empty in spite of the early hour and damp weather. The sole occupant was a big gnarly snapping turtle occupied with laying eggs in the loose gravel at the edge. I took this for a good omen, snapped a few pictures from a safe distance, and left her to her business.

Kal splashed through the shallows, chasing sunfish and minnows while I unloaded the boat and grabbed the last few things from the cab. I pushed off without getting my feet wet but got soaked when the dog hopped over the gunwale and promptly did the "Wet Labrador Shake," drenching the boat and its contents from stem to stern. With that over, we were off, trolling along the pine and aspen jungle of the shoreline. I sat in the stern seat gripping the motor handle while weaving in and out along the weed line, prospecting for fish with a crankbait dragging behind. Kal balanced in the middle with her front feet up on the gunwale. We weren't the only ones out on the water. Halfway around the lake a pair of curious loons swam out to greet us, following us for most of the first lap.

Trolling the crankbait didn't work any magic so I killed the gas motor and drifted along the shore, slowly bumping the boat along with the electric motor. A cast with a small feather jig into the weeds brought the first fish of the day—a small feisty pumpkinseed sunfish colored in tropical orange and green. After a few more of them, I switched to a floating minnow lure and soon caught an eighteen-inch largemouth bass that jumped twice and tried to toss the lure back at me.

I continued this pace for several hours, alternating trolling with the big motor to locate big fish, then coasting along the shore with the electric motor, prospecting for sunnies and crappies. Two northern pike couldn't resist the crankbaits. One nice five-pounder dove deep and had to be winched up from the bottom tangled in a clump of weeds that weighed more than it did. Small crappies and sunfish continued to attack my jig any time it was plopped down into the bulrushes and pond weeds close to shore. This wasn't high-tech trophy fishing. It was just pure, simple fun.

No other human fishermen showed up to share the misty lake. The loons kept watch, diving to fish for themselves, and hooting softly to each other. We coasted up to a doe deer, clad in her red summer coat, wading ankle-deep in the shallows while grazing head down on some tasty greens. I was hoping to spot a tiny spotted fawn hiding back in the undergrowth, but Kal considers deer filthy animals of the worst kind and couldn't resist letting go with a burst of echoing barks, sending the deer crashing off, white tail flying high. A lone eagle silently cruised across the lake and an osprey wheeled above us, riding the air on hinged wings while watching for any injured fish we might leave behind.

By mid-morning, I was out of snacks and coffee and Kal was restless despite a quick shore break on an island. The loons got restless too. One took a run across the lake, its wings rhythmically slapping the water until it reached lift-off and gained enough altitude to circle the shore. I considered leaving too. Then the loon returned, coasting back into the lake from on high, timing its landing with a long smooth belly slide into the water. Maybe I wasn't quite ready to leave either. I made a final lap, working the shore for another half-hour and was rewarded with two scrappy, toothy northern pike to admire and release.

There was no need to hurry back at the landing—no other impatient boaters jockeying for position while learning how to back boat trailers. I took my time loading the boat and organizing it for the bumpy ride home. Kal hopped back in the truck, did the obligatory shake to coat the inside with a fine mist, and we headed back through the forest.

A mile up the road, we met an old four-door Pontiac pulling a similar red Lund. The driver pulled over to let me pass on the one-lane road and rolled down a window to talk. A thirty-five-ish guy with glasses and an old baseball cap hung out the window while a teenaged boy and girl peered out from behind him. "Got your limit already?" he asked.

"Nope," I replied. "I caught a bunch but I let them all go for you." This guy didn't look like much of a threat to the fish population. So I filled in a few details, telling him where the sunfish were bedded and what lures might get him and the kids a nice northern or two to brag about.

"Better hurry!" I added as we parted. "There's no one else out there. You can pretend you own the whole lake." I drove off into the mist feeling good about myself. It wasn't even noon and I had already topped off a good day with a good deed. And I still had time for a nap.

Adventures in Forestry

Adventures in Forestry

On an unseasonably warm April morning, some twenty years ago, teenaged son Steve and I labored to plant two hundred red pines, spruce, and balsam fir on our untamed five acres. Planting trees among trees on what the Realtor had called a "heavily wooded acreage" might seem strange. My thought was that the mainly mature deciduous forest needed a little variety, some young trees, and a practical evergreen screening from the closest neighbor's cabin site. We spaded the little one-foot tall seedlings into random groups, worked up a good sweat, and left the trees to grow while we went fishing.

And grow they did. The survival rate was high for the next two years with favorable weather conditions and a low deer population. The red pines and spruce were reaching three feet in height with the balsams struggling somewhat when the winter of '95/'96 came along. Forty below, snow up past a Sasquatch's butt, and a hungry growing deer population. The deer never thanked me for the smorgasbord planted for them. Didn't even offer up one of their own as a sacrifice during deer season. They chomped down nearly every one of the two hundred fledgling trees and then moved on to the neighbors—who had done the same thing. Thus began my trial and error experimentation in Northwoods forestry. So far as I can tell, only one lonely spruce remains of that original two hundred.

I've learned a few things via experimentation since then. Deer have an order of preference when it

25

comes to edible evergreens. They will eat white pine and white cedar first, balsam fir next, then move on to the Norway or red pine. Spruce seem to be the last on their menu—only resorted to when things get real rough. Protective measures can be taken on a small scale. Fencing individual trees, capping the top bud with a paper cap, and/or using a stinky deterrent spray will slow the damage. None of these is perfect. Individual fencing is labor-intensive and expensive. The caps likewise take a lot of time and labor and always seem to fall off in late winter—just when the deer are the hungriest. The expensive spray works sometimes, if you remember to keep reapplying it every month or so.

As far as trees go, leafy deciduous trees are even harder to grow. They are harder to bud cap, sprays don't stick as well, and what could be tastier than a nice maple or apple tree? Deer can cause problems with these whether eating away from the top down or roughly pruning side branches for snacks. Other critters like them too. There are two kinds of tree-eating rabbits at our place and at least two types of bark-eating, tree-girdling mice, along with the occasional woodchuck/ground hog. I haven't caught the latter hassling my trees yet but I have my suspicions.

One other critter can also cause problems if you aren't careful. Not many people would consider the black bear a threat to trees. They would probably worry about their own skin first. My neighbor Tom would disagree. He fertilized a prime specimen right in front of his cabin with a tried and true method supposedly used by Native Americans long before Columbus and the Pilgrims. The weekend's fish guts were buried and a nice, expensive nursery-grown spruce was planted on top of them. The local bear waited until Tom left, then dug the tree up, tossed it aside, and helped himself to the "fertilizer." Mr. Bruin chose not to replant the tree.

Given these years of experience, here's a few suggestions. Put razor wire prison fence around a few precious white and Norway pines in prime locations. Then plant a lot of spruce elsewhere and hope for about ten years of mild winters. I would also give some free advice to any neighbors and maybe even help them plant large numbers of white pines, red pines, maples, and apples to decoy the deer in their direction.

Just don't get too cocky. As I found out, a rutting buck deer in October can take on a prized ten-foot spruce and kill it dead while using it as a convenient antler-rubbing spot. And while I am handing out free advice, please consider taking up deer hunting. You won't be able to make much of a dent in the local population given modern big game hunting regulations. But revenge in this case can taste sweet when grilled over charcoal and served medium rare with a little wild mushroom cream sauce.

Legends of the Fire

Loud laughter woke me just past 5 a.m. on a Saturday morning. I dragged myself out of the cozy sleeping bag and groggily stumbled downstairs to the cabin's lower level by the dim light of a June sunrise. The laughter came to an abrupt halt as I opened the back screen door. The six young men seated around the campfire turned in unison at the sound of the door. My two sons and my eldest sister's four shared the same guilty look. The two Labrador Retrievers sleeping at their feet snored on oblivious to the interruption.

"Keep it down, boys. Some of us are still trying to sleep."

The heads nodded in unison. I shook mine and headed back upstairs for a couple more hours in the sleeping bag. Midnight had been my limit last night. The six cousins had continued on, pulling an all-nighter at the fire without me.

I knew what had kept them up. This bunch had grown up together and shared many outdoor vacation adventures in the process. While girls, cars, hunting and fishing were surely mentioned during the night, I'm also sure many stories from their joint vacation adventures were retold and embellished.

Like the camping trip to Madeleine Island on the Wisconsin side of Lake Superior. Rain, cold, wind, and huge slimy slugs crawling on tents were the highlights of the trip for the adults. These guys were more likely to remember sneaking away from the confining rules of parents to flirt with the massive waves crashing over the rocks, beachcombing when the sun came out on the last day, or the Fourth of July fireworks over the island's harbor. Then there was the car ferry trip across to the island.

Son Steve likely said to older brother Andy —"Remember when I was scared as hell that the ferry boat would sink? Dad said 'Nah, these never sink.' Then you had to add in, 'Well, then why is it named the Nichevo II?'"

I'm sure they talked about one of our week-long trips to Itasca State Park—the year the raccoons were trying to take over the campground. "Remember that pair of baby coons that spent the day hiding in the wheel well of Dad's truck?"

"Yeah—they raided the cooler, punched holes in all our juice boxes and tried to suck them dry. And then one stole the bacon from the lady camping next to us. She was chasing him around the campground yelling 'He's got the bacon! He's got the bacon!'"

Also likely retold was the tale of Grandpa and the outhouse. "And how about when Grandpa went to the outhouse at Bear Head Park and dropped his checkbook in? I thought I would die laughing when he got his fishing pole and went jigging for it."

"How about all the one-liners we came up with that night?" a nephew might add. "My favorite had to be 'Grandpa, isn't the fishing kind of crappy in that spot?'"

"No!" one of my sons would cut in—"My favorite was 'Grandpa, I hear the fishing stinks here!'"

The lesson for Grandpa at the time, other than not to drop your checkbook in an outhouse, was not to do so when there's six young grandsons with fertile minds hanging around. Going to the outhouse has since been referred to as "Goin' to the bank" by this bunch.

I snuggled down into my sleeping bag and lay awake eavesdropping, curious to see where the conversation would pick back up. The story of the mouse that jumped into the campfire ring and perished with all hands watching? The storm that dumped a foot of rain and numerous trees all around our tents? Maybe a few tall fishing tales with me as the guide where the fish got bigger and more numerous?

It wasn't long. Son Andy opened the silence —"Remember when Dad left Mom's Jeep in gear while we were packing for vacation and got out to check the trailer? It pulled the boat right down the driveway and banged into his car. I thought she was going to kill him!"

Then came son Steve's turn—"Did you hear what he did on Memorial Weekend? He forgot to put the plug in the big boat and sank it at the dock while he and Mom were having supper. Took them hours to get it floating again!"

The others howled with laughter and begged for more details. I pulled my sleeping bag up over my ears and burrowed down in. You make one little mistake and suddenly a legend is born. And there are some legends you just don't want to be part of.

The Perfect Crime

It was a dark and stormy night outside my cozy cabin. The inside temperature dropped as wind howled and snow rattled off windows. I got up from my chair and added another piece of hand-split, free-range, locally grown, organic, air-dried oak to the cheery blaze in the woodstove, then sat back down to the computer to ponder the perfect crime.

Last summer I ran short of firewood and started thinking about winter—winter without firewood and heat at my rustic weekend retreat. Without firewood, there would be no ice fishing on Crooked Lake, no cross-country skiing with the dog, no quiet nights with the woodstove warming my back as I wrote. It might drive a law-abiding man to a life of crime.

A fallen oak on neighboring property tempted me. The mighty trunk had splintered in a thunderstorm and crashed down to the forest floor. There it lay on uninhabited foreclosed property, wasting away while legal matters were resolved in a faraway place. It was a victimless crime waiting to happen. And if there was a victim, it was me, since I had paid for years of snowplowing and gravel hauling on the shared driveway with no help from the vanished neighbor.

So, supposing I was ready to commit a misdeed in the name of warmth, how would I pull off the caper without ending up in the local jail or at the very least in the headlines of the local newspaper? It was more complicated than it sounds and, for all I know, firewood theft could be a capital offense in the

Northwoods, like stealing a horse in the Old West.

Logistics would be one problem. The tree was over two feet in diameter and lay fifty yards off the driveway in thick brush. It would need to be cut into manageable pieces and hauled out bit by bit. However, once done, the thick summer greenery would hide the crime scene for months. The new owners would never know it had been there.

Chainsaw noise was an obvious issue. No one has yet invented a stealth chainsaw. I'd have to choose my best saw, make sure it was full of gas and oil, get the dang thing to start, and then cut like crazy before someone investigated. I don't have many neighbors, but the ones I have are nosy, know the property lines, and might not be able to keep quiet.

Another threat might be a tourist from the resort down the road, out for a walk with a curious mutt. I could wear my camouflage hunting clothes and mask to hide from a walker. The dog would be more of a problem. Some friendly Labrador or Golden Retriever might smell me and come crashing into the woods, tail wagging, happy to make a new friend. A camo-clad, masked guy wielding a chainsaw might look a little suspicious to the Master. A call to the local authorities, neighbors, or the Sheriff's Department could spell trouble.

There would be other dangers. Any crime show watcher knows that something is bound to go wrong. My saw could refuse to start, run out of gas, or get stuck in the tree at a critical moment. Any of those would be bad enough. It would likely be the loud swearing on my part that could draw in those curious neighbors. Or maybe I would break a leg stepping in a woodchuck hole and have to call for help. Or even have the tree crush me in an unhandy moment. There's a headline for you—"Local Cabin Owner Flattened By Tree While Stealing Firewood." Also possible was that my old trailer would break an axle and leave a trailer load of purloined wood blocking the driveway for all to see.

Then there's the age-old problem of leaving evidence at the scene of the crime. It's not likely that local law enforcement would spend much time investigating a stolen dead tree, even if it was reported. However, I have been known to lose things, even when not stressed out in the midst of questionable activity. A misplaced glove, a lost coffee cup, or a piece of broken trailer taillight might make solving this misdeed too easy and tempt them to haul me in just to pad year-end statistics. I'd have to be careful about loading the trailer too. A series of road-killed logs or leaking sawdust leaving a Hansel and Gretel style trail back to the cabin wouldn't be good.

My problems wouldn't end once the wood was back to the cabin's yard. More chainsaw work and the sweaty job of splitting the mess would take time. And speaking of nosy persons, my wife was bound to take interest. "Where'd you get the wood?" she'd ask.

"Back in the woods," I'd answer evasively.

"Oh, when did you stop at the DNR office and get the firewood permit?" she would persist.

"I didn't. This is from private land—not the forest," I'd reply.

"Our land?" she might ask, again a bit too nosy for her own good.

"No," I'd say, voice dripping with sarcasm. "Not ours—the neighbors!"

Maybe that would get her to back off in time for me to finish cutting, splitting, stacking, and covering before anyone else showed up and started the same line of questioning. I'd hate to have to make someone "disappear" just to cover up the theft of a little firewood.

I got up and added another piece of hand-split, free-range, locally grown, organic, air-dried oak to the woodstove. Yes, this could be the perfect crime, especially once all the evidence has gone up in smoke.

Trail Cam

Contrary to the grainy night vision images shown on Reality TV, and the opinions expressed by the highly paid stars of the shows, I have some doubts about whether or not Big Foot lives. If he does live, he must be rare in my neck of the woods. This belief is based in part on the vast knowledge I acquired in receiving a degree in Biology, a Master Naturalist Certification, and from roaming these woods for over fifty years without a firsthand encounter. But the main source of my doubt is the fact that Mr. or Mrs. Sasquatch have yet to show up on one of the many trail cameras stashed in the woods around my cabin.

Let me digress for a minute in case you don't know what a trail camera is. Somewhere around twenty years ago, an enterprising electronic genius figured out how to hook up a motion sensor to a camera and weatherproof the whole apparatus. Trail cam was born. Take one out in the woods, set it up overlooking a trail or a food source, and walk away to let it record pictures of whatever critters walk the trail or stop by for a snack.

The first ones were based on old fashioned 35mm film cameras and powered by bulky nine-volt lantern batteries. They were slow to catch on—at least with those of us who consider money to be an issue. The batteries were expensive, didn't last long, and you had to pay for film and film processing. Thus twenty-four pictures of a branch, waving in the wind in front of the camera, set you back about twenty dollars. Then technology caught up. You can now buy a decent digital camera with an infrared flash for under a hundred bucks. They run for most of a year on regular household batteries. You can even hook one up to a mini-solar panel and not worry about losing power. Download the pictures off the camera's storage card to your computer and delete the megapixels off into the ozone (or wherever deleted megapixels actually go) if you don't like them.

The cameras are especially popular with deer hunters who use them to determine if a trophy buck is leaving those big tracks or just Bambi with size fourteen hoofs. They will take pictures of anything that trips the motion sensor, providing proof of the wide variety of wildlife that clandestinely roams the State Forest surrounding my cabin. My cameras have captured flying squirrels flying, raccoons raiding, porcupines prowling, skunks stinking, deer from Bambi to buck, bobcats, bears, and birds of every feather. In other words, I have pictures of just about all the critters that are supposed to inhabit these woods— except "Big Feet."

Trail cams aren't just for the forest either. Want a close-up picture of that beautiful grosbeak that's visiting your birdfeeder? Get a trail cam and set it up on a tripod overlooking the feeder. Wonder what sort of varmint is leaving that mess on the end of the dock every night? Strap a trail cam to a dock post and make sure the flash is turned on. You could even hide one on the porch by the beer fridge and figure out who or what is emptying it when you aren't around.

Just be mindful that sometimes ignorance is bliss. The cameras will probably show things you didn't want to see and confirm the existence of creatures you may have hoped didn't share the neighborhood. The high resolution color camera might catch the neighbor's dog leaving a present on the lawn. Or maybe you don't want to prove that bears roam the cabin grounds if your spouse is a bit squeamish about large furry wildlife with big pointy teeth. And finally, I could be wrong. Maybe Big Foot does live in your neck of the woods. If he does, do you really want to see a picture of him skinny-dipping off the dock at midnight?

Monsters of the Deep

The dog and I arrived at the cabin late on a summer evening. It can get real dark and spooky in the woods on a moonless summer night. Still, I felt compelled to open a beer, grab a flashlight, and wander down to the dock to slow down from the stress of the three-hour drive and soak up a bit of Northwoods ambiance before bed. I pulled up a lawn chair on the end of the dock and sat back, listening to the sunfish smacking bugs in the lily pads and the loons serenading the rapid passing of summer. The dog was a quiet presence beside me.

This peaceful interlude was interrupted by a commotion along the shore of Big Island, one hundred yards away across the channel. Some thing or things, some large thing or things, started grunting, splashing, clunking, wheezing, and struggling in the shallow weedy water. I strained to listen, trying to pick up a hint of what was happening. The dog had the same reaction. She listened intently, head cocked, alert, silent, not willing to challenge the perpetrator with her usual throaty bark or even a low warning growl.

The dim beam of my flashlight was no help. It could not cut through the dark of that much night. The racket continued on for ten minutes or more while I mulled possibilities. An asthmatic bear, caught fishing at the edge of the island, and struggling to climb the steep bank? Beavers wrestling a log, having bitten off more than they could chew? A geriatric buck deer, clanging antlers off trees as he struggled to climb the slippery shore? All these and more were considered and checked off as not likely. When the splashing, wheezing, grunting, clunking abruptly ended, I had no clue. Leaving many unanswered questions behind, the dog and I climbed the hill to the cabin and locked the doors, having had enough mystery, intrigue, and Northwoods ambiance for one dark night.

It took several years to solve that mystery. Recently, on another late summer day, this time in broad daylight, I was hiking a trail that hugged the shore of a small lake. While I was pausing to enjoy a scenic overlook, a loud splashing, wheezing, grunting, clunking commotion started in the water below—an exact replica of what occurred on that dark night.

At the bottom of the steep bank, two snapping turtles were squared off. Big snapping turtles, shells that looked a foot and a half wide, the size and type of which you dare not think about when skinny-dipping off the dock in the moonlight. The two were locked in what seemed like mortal combat, wrestling shell to shell, hook-jawed snapper mouth to hook-jawed snapper mouth, clawing, kicking, scratching, and all the while wheezing and grunting like a pair of oxygen-challenged miniature Godzillas. They would unlock and back off, a foot apart in the shallow water, eyeing each other suspiciously. Then one would charge (if you can imagine a slow motion turtle charge), bang into the other, and again the water-splashing, mud-flying struggle would be on.

Territorial squabble? Fight over tasty bit of dead frog or stinky fish? A fight between two behemoth males over some long gone but attractive, demure female? I watched, not betting on the outcome.

The end came rather abruptly. They separated and one appeared to surrender, laying motionless, half-floating, half-grounded near shore. Then the purpose of the "fight" became clear. The winner moved to the rear of the subdued beast and mounted its gnarly shell. It was time to reevaluate. This had not been a fight to the death between two rival males over territory, food, or a prospective mate. It was the exact opposite, a complex mating ritual, perhaps meant to satisfy the female with the worth and strength of the male.

I later researched snapping turtles via the usual reliable Internet sources, confirmed the incident, and learned a bit more. It seems that snapping turtles can and, from my experiences, do mate anywhere from spring to fall. The females practice something I will term "delayed conception," somehow preventing their eggs from being fertilized for many months, thus assuring they can be laid at an opportune time to increase the survival rate of the offspring. The eggs can lay dormant over the winter and hatch next year. Late fall hatching baby turtles may even spend the winter in the burrow dug for the eggs. This explains another mystery—why I have found baby snappers hatching in all warm seasons of the year.

I'd be doing snappers a disservice if I didn't add more info. Their scientific name is "Chelydra serpentine." The "serpentine" part translates to "snake-like," given the look of their pointy not-so-little heads. They can grow to close to eighty pounds and live for many decades, maybe even a century. They usually are not as fierce as their reputation. Most spend lives hunting and scavenging in lakes and ponds and don't go looking for trouble. However, I liked Wikipedia's advice on one issue I hadn't even considered—"The common snapping turtle is not an ideal pet." That's good advice to follow since they do have strong, fast jaws and don't like to be messed with when on land laying eggs or traveling between water sources. Given my experience, I'd also stay away from them during mating time.

Wheelin' and Dealin'

Craft shops? Antique stores? Seasonal boutiques? Yes, the North Country is full of these, offering up everything from exquisite handmade pottery to cheap T-shirts advertising favorite resorts and lakes. Good places all, ready and eager to part money from tourists. But for the real deals on real good stuff, along with side helpings of adventure, history, and a big slice of Americana, get off Main Street and into the flea markets, garage sales, and community celebrations.

Start with the flea markets if you're squeamish about walking up to a stranger's house and wandering around in their garage. That's what we did one recent weekend. With time on our hands and a loosely organized bunch of friends and relatives hanging around, we caravanned down the road to the open-air summer bazaar just east of Park Rapids.

This place has everything. Need cheap toys, flashlights, or pocket knives to keep the kids happy and occupied on a rainy day in the resort cabin? Got it—by the truckload. In fact, how does that vendor guy fit everything back into one small truck? If I ever need to move, he'll be the one to call. Want fresh fruits, veggies, homemade bread, cookies, and jelly? Got it—along with fishing lures, old tools, boxes of paperback books, vinyl records, and small appliances that were popular forty years ago.

The guys pushing wares from behind the flea market tables are real pros, shameless hucksters all—

probably used car salesmen moonlighting on days off. Overheard snatches of sales pitches: "I could get $150 bucks for that at the auction, but for you, today, I'll take fifty."

"Hey, nice duck decoys, eh? That's not the original paint—a friend of mine touches them up in his shop. I'll sell the pair for $40. It cost me more than that to have them repainted."

"Like that lure? Great trout lure—I caught a four-pound brook trout with it in a little secret lake up the Gunflint Trail last year." I'm tempted to step in and offer the guy ten dollars for the name of the trout lake. I have plenty of lures.

Marcie and I cautiously examine the wares, avoid eye contact with the sales guys, and make a few strategic purchases. I get a small antique ice saw (or so I think) for ten bucks. She settles on a couple of used books for fifty cents each and five old license plates for the collection lining the walls of the outhouse. Included in the twenty dollar "buy four/get one free" deal are a rare Ontario plate and a colorful one from Utah. We call it quits before we run out of cash and leave before testing the cuisine at the food booth.

The fun has just begun. Saturday is the official garage sale day in Nevis. Every other house seems to have a sale, with churches and businesses pitching in with fund raisers and sidewalk sales. We hit the Lutheran Church first for coffee, iced cinnamon rolls, and deals. I score two used paperbacks and a heavy-duty fry pan. Fifty cents apiece. Then it's on to the side streets and the real garages.

The sales pitches here are less direct and delivered with less pressure than the flea market. In fact, no pressure some times. I look over a brand name mountain bike, consider the three dollar price tag, and debate a low ball offer. The lady-of-the-sale walks up and beats me to the punch. "If you want it, take it, free, no charge to a good home." She's obviously not a moonlighting flea market salesperson. In fact, I feel cheap and guilty. Marcie is not as lucky. A pair of newly reupholstered chairs catch her eye. The sticky note price tag says "$75." There's no high-pressure sales pitch from this garage sale lady. She's firm—sort of. Her bottom-line price is $60 and she doesn't claim that the reupholstering cost her $200. I wave down a passing friend and load them in his pickup. Free delivery even.

We hop from neighborhood to neighborhood and walk the streets of bargains. Things start to add up. A huge shed deer antler for one dollar. Don't know what will be done with it but it is a huge deer antler, for only a buck. A pair of rod holders for the fishing boat takes a five dollar bill from my cash stash but would have cost forty in a retail store. Next a camo folding chair with swivel seat catches my eye. "How much?" I ask the pony-tailed, army-fatigue-clothed proprietor.

"Three bucks," he says.

"Sold!" says I.

"Damn!" he says. "Knew I should have said five!"

Marcie scores a few more books, some pizza plates, miscellaneous housewares, and a plastic berry-picking basket. We reluctantly pass on a pop-up camper trailer, a boat or two, a smoker, and other items too numerous to mention. Then comes a real gem.

Tucked in the back corner of a big storage shed is a table full of beer glasses, most sporting labels

of brands long gone. Oly, Blatz, Stroh's, Old Style—
the beers of my wasted youth, before that trip to
Europe turned me on to real beer. At a buck apiece, I
can't resist a piece of my history. I buy five to
begin with and then go back for ten more at the text
mail urging of my oldest son. A young lady behind the
card table carefully wraps them in old newspaper.
"They were my grandpa's collection," she says sadly.
"But he's gone and we can't keep everything."

We retreat to the cabin to unload and unwind.
After two days of shopping you would think we were
done until Black Friday. Nope. The weekend brings one
last chance at bargains. Sunday is "Taste of Dorset."
The restaurants in this tiny burg line the streets
with food booths for one August Sunday afternoon. It's
mandatory you eat and drink until you can eat and
drink no more, and then spend a dollar for a write-in
vote to nominate yourself as mayor.

It's also mandatory to put in a bid at the local
church's fundraiser—a silent auction that includes a
mixture of Grandma's old Depression glass, artwork by
local artists, and small well-used household goods of
questionable age. The rules are simple. Write your
name and bid on the sheet next to the item and hope no
one else wants it as bad as you before the appointed
closing time. Strategy is important. Really want
something? Show them you mean business! Blow the
competition away with a big bid—say five dollars
instead of the minimum one. Then have more to eat and
drink and check back later to see if someone has one-
dollar-upped you.

The best deals come right at the end—the orphan
stuff no one has placed a bid on. In this case there's
a set of nice wicker baskets. They're mine for the one

dollar minimum just as the auction closes. A decorative collector plate also catches my eye. White porcelain, eight inches or so, with an old Scandinavian church scene etched in silver gray. "Roros" it says under the scene and "Porsgrund Norway" on the back. It's worth a dollar just to find out where it came from. I snatch it up and hand over a dollar to the church-lady-in-charge. Treasure or junk? Only time and a little research will tell.

Once it's all done, we spread out the loot from the three-day shopping orgy on the deck and take stock. There are some regrets—all bargains that were passed on. Marcie wishes we could have sprung for the camper trailer. An ornate lime green Depression glass pitcher and four glasses makes my list. But at $25 and too fragile for cabin life, passing on it was the safe thing to do. I should have bought the whole collection of beer glasses.

Included free of charge is the education. My Dad stops by for a visit and picks up the ice saw. "Haven't seen a hay saw in years," he says. "I forgot all about them." He turns it over in his hands, reflecting, remembering days of hard work many moons ago.

"Are you sure it's not an ice saw?" I ask.

"Nope," he says. "You used this to cut slabs out of hay stacked by hand the old fashioned way." I'll trust him on this and whether it's an ice saw or hay saw, it is a neat piece of Americana.

The Scandinavian plate turns out to be the biggest treasure. A quick Internet search shows "Roros" is a Norwegian mountain mining town famous for the old church and bell tower pictured on the plate. And "Porsgrund" is a noted Scandinavian porcelain manufacturer. A quick look at Internet auction sites shows similar plates listed for as much as fifteen dollars. How's that for a potential 1500 percent return on investment?

It also gets me thinking, while surveying the pile of treasures spread out before me. Considering what's already stashed in the storage shed, in the cabin, and back home, it's high time for a flea market booth or garage sale of our own.

Aunt Mickey's Rhubarb

It had been a tough spring for our old rhubarb plant. First the warm weather of March coaxed it into peeking above the garden mulch way too early. Then the predictable April cold snap froze those tender young shoots back to ground level. That hadn't worried me too much. Rhubarb is a hardy plant and this particular one had been around awhile.

My Aunt Mickey had dug the plant from her western Minnesota garden close to thirty years ago and presented it to us. I don't remember the specific reason. It might have been a house-warming gift or she simply might have thought that any young couple of Scandinavian heritage should have a rhubarb plant in their garden. But now the plant had been hacked to pieces by my wife in a gardening frenzy while I was off on a fishing trip. One small portion had been moved to a planter on the edge of the garden. The rest lay shriveled and dying in the compost pile.

Marcie was unrepentant. "It was in the wrong spot—it had to go! Besides, it will be fine—you can't kill that rhubarb!" Behind her stood my oldest sister, one of her best friends, mortified at what had happened. She was clutching a small remnant of the plant, a sad and wilted fragment, salvaged from the compost.

"I'll take this one home and find a spot for it," she said, clearly understanding the history and family ties to the butchered plant and the severity of the offense.

Since the deed had been done, I decided to make the best of it and keep quiet for the time being. Once the women left, I clandestinely salvaged the hacked-up pieces from the compost pile and planted the half a dozen small clumps on the outlot behind our garden fence. I didn't need that many rhubarb plants but I couldn't see letting it go to waste. Within the week, two more shoots poked through in the location of the old plant and were quickly moved before Marcie spotted them. And then I found two more somehow clinging to life in the compost pile. So, I ended up with a new fifteen-foot row of rhubarb in addition to the new old plant, which actually seemed to be doing fine. I added a little fertilizer and mulch to the transplants and waited to see what would happen.

My curiosity led me to doing a little Internet research while I waited. As usual, once you start on the Internet, one thing leads to another. Like the history of rhubarb. I had always assumed that it was a northern European plant, perhaps a native Scandinavian, cultivated simply because nothing else would grow in frost-plagued soil. Wrong, at least according to the wiseness of the Internet. Seems like it probably originated in the Far East and slowly traveled westward along the trade routes. The Internet also alternatively warned of the toxic nature of its leaves and praised its long known medicinal properties. An ancient Chinese cure for cancer? A little known Viking love potion? Nope—supposedly the leaves are a great laxative if used in the right amount. Personally, this is one organic herbal "cure" I won't be trying at home.

I also assumed that it was something reserved for pies, desserts, homemade wine, and other sweet delights. Wrong again. According to the Foodie websites, it appears there was a rhubarb revelation several years ago—rhubarb and fish were at least a minor craze. Somehow I had missed that in spite of many hours spent watching cooking and gardening shows during the winter. But since I am always looking for new twists on fish, I gave the rhubarb sauce for fish a try.

Many websites offered up the same generic recipe with only minor variations. So I came up with my own take based on what was available. I bought a small bunch of de-leafed reddish-green stalks at the local Farmers Market since my own plants needed to recuperate before harvesting. Yes, I paid for rhubarb. That has to be a major sin in Scandinavian culture, almost as bad as paying for a zucchini. I am sure Aunt Mickey would have had something to say about that.

I chopped up a couple stalks of rhubarb, a carrot, a shallot, and an onion, and sautéed the mix in butter. I then added white wine and clam juice and simmered it a bit before blending everything to "smooth" in my food processor. The result was a creamy light orange-colored sauce with a definite tang. It was a nice compliment to a piece of grilled salmon. Think for a minute—it makes sense. What other seasoning do you use on fish to enhance the flavor? Maybe some sour lemon juice? Think of rhubarb sauce in the same way—something to add a tart spark to fish.

As for other more traditional rhubarb recipes, there's no need for experimentation as far as I am concerned. Just consult the real experts. I reach for one of the many church fund-raiser cookbooks on my kitchen shelf. Trust me here on two things. There will be a rhubarb section if it's a Minnesota church cookbook, and you can't go wrong with a church lady recipe. I used the rest of my "boughten" rhubarb on a rhubarb coffee cake recipe from one of them. It passed the test at work. The entire pan disappeared from the break room table by noon.

It does look like I am going to need plenty of recipes. Every one of the clones that resulted from Marcie's garden hack job appears to be thriving and ready to produce a bumper crop. Maybe she was right for once. You really can't kill Aunt Mickey's rhubarb.

Fish Sauce Recipe
- *Finely chopped rhubarb—about a cup and a half*
- *One small carrot—chopped*
- *One shallot—chopped*
- *One medium onion—chopped*
- *One tablespoon of unsalted butter*
- *Half a cup of white wine*
- *One cup clam juice*

Sauté rhubarb and veggies in butter at low heat until soft (ten minutes). Add the wine and clam juice. Simmer for fifteen minutes. Blend smooth in food processor. Reheat at low temperature and spoon over grilled or baked fish.

A Walk in the Woods
—Foraying With the Paul Bunyan Mushroom Club

On an overcast August morning, I prepared for what many people would consider to be a very dangerous assignment. I armed myself with bug repellant, sunscreen, and a woven wicker basket decorated with a green floral design. I then headed north on the back roads of the Paul Bunyan State Forest on the hunt for "Cantharellus cibarius"—the wild chanterelle mushroom.

It's hard to find a person that doesn't look a bit frightened when you mention collecting and actually eating wild mushrooms. Even magazine editors. When I posed the story idea to one of my favorite editors, her response was typical—"Wild mushrooms? They scare me!" Well, folks, it doesn't have to be that way—at least when you can tap into the collective knowledge of an experienced group of people like I was about to meet—the regulars of the Paul Bunyan Mushroom Club.

I had been on several other mushroom hunts (or "forays" as club members call them), so I knew the drill. I followed emailed directions to a clearing on the edge of the Paul Bunyan State Forest. Waiting there amongst the mud puddles from last night's torrential thunder storm were several familiar faces— John Mikesh, Rosa Stolzenberg, and Paula Peters.

The Paul Bunyan Mushroomers are a loosely organized group. The core members got together over twenty years ago, united in their interest of collecting and identifying wild mushrooms—and eating them when appropriate. The core members take turns heading up forays throughout late spring, summer, and early fall. A typical season might have nine forays.

Paula was the designated leader for this outing. I talked with her while we waited for others to show. Paula says that morel mushrooms are popular because they are tasty and easy to identify. But they are only the start to the mushroom season for her and other experienced mushroomers. Morels are targeted in early May to early June. The group then moves on to chanterelles in midsummer and Chicken of the Woods in late summer and into early October. Foray participants can also expect to find oyster mushrooms, lobster mushrooms, the occasional black trumpet, Bolites, Hen of the Woods (my favorite), and a host of other interesting finds that range from simply inedible to nasty poisonous.

More people arrived while we talked until a varied group of over twenty people was assembled around us. Some were hard core regulars. About half were new or, like me, casual hangers-on that make it when they can. Women were well represented, and so were brightly dressed children as young as five years old. Paula says that typical forays include about twenty to thirty people with about half being regulars and the other half new people or occasional participants like me.

After some quick introductions, Paula offered the group basic instructions and advice. Today's target was the chanterelle, an apricot- or peach-colored trumpet-shaped mushroom featured in many gourmet cooking shows and popular worldwide. While the focus was to harvest chanterelles and other edibles, Paula instructed the group on how to properly collect specimens of any mushrooms for identification later.

Part of the material that the mushroom was growing on or in should remain attached to the base. Paula explained that this material can be an important key to identification—some mushrooms grow in soil, some in rotting wood, others straight from the sides of standing trees. The underground parts of a mushroom can also assist in identification. Pocket knives such as my ever-present real Swiss army knife can be used to assist in this process.

This instructional session is where you also learn one of the most important rules of mushrooming etiquette—no plastic bags please! These are handy and often the container of choice for newcomers. However, their airtight confined spaces lead to quick decay of mushrooms. A much better option is a paper or net bag, an open ice cream bucket or, better yet and much more fashionable, a wicker or woven basket. I made the plastic bag mistake on my first foray. That's why I was now sporting that cute woven basket with the green floral design mentioned earlier.

Her initial instructions complete, Paula offered options. We could either strike out on our own or follow one of the regulars for further hands-on instruction and identification assistance. Two toots of the whistle she carried in her foray kit would recall us to the clearing after an hour or so of mushrooming.

Having followed John around on other forays, I was looking for something different and saw an opportunity. Laura, Molly, and Jack (5 ½, 6 ½, and 8 ½ years old respectively), were brightly dressed, equipped with their own ice cream pails, and hanging out with their Grandmother Helen. I hung close to the kids and Helen, got to know them a bit, and took a few background photos. I then branched out looking for a chanterelle hotspot.

Luck and a bit of experience were on my side. In a patch of tall Norway pines, I found a modest group of about eight chanterelles—their apricot color distinctive and contrasting with the dried brown pine needles and leaves they were poking up through. I took a few photos and then called for Laura, Molly, and Jack. As expected, my new little friends descended on the chanterelles like candy tossed from a parade float. A few got trampled in the rush. Most ended up in their personal pails with only a bit of polite sibling rivalry.

I might add here that you should never be afraid to take well-behaved kids mushrooming. Once they know what to look for, their sharp young eyes and their enthusiasm are a great combination. It also helps that they are shorter, closer to the ground and the mushrooms.

Having established my mushroomer credentials, the youngsters, their Grandmother, and I continued wandering in a loose group. The hour passed quickly. We found mushrooms in general to be scarce. The weather had been dry and they hadn't yet had a chance to take advantage of last night's downpour. We did manage to find a few interesting odds and ends to put in our baskets and pails. We might have found more but we discovered another bonus of being out in the woods in August. The youngsters and I found several good raspberry patches loaded with ripe red berries and got a bit distracted . . .

We had covered only a tiny bit of the thousands of acres of State forest when Paula's whistle echoed through the woods, signaling the end of the hunt and summoning us back to the clearing. It was time for the next phase of the foray—mushroom show and tell. Members of the groups emerged from the forest, converged on the folding tables Paula had set up, and the fun and chatter began. Most of the group had the same limited success but a wide assortment of mushroom shapes and colors were soon spread out on the tables. It should be mentioned that John, being the expert he is, did score about twenty chanterelles, along with a few other interesting finds.

As old and young clustered about, Paula, Rosa, John, and some of the other regulars helped us sort and identify our finds. They provided reference books to assist with difficult specimens. Even with these books, they relied heavily on years of hands-on experience to show us the edible from the simply interesting and/or dangerous. The best pictures can't show all the small subtleties and variations present in separate mushrooms of the same type. In addition to the chanterelles, John showed us other edibles including a bright orange gnarly lobster mushroom named for its lobster- or crab-like odor and color.

While Paula and the other leaders continued to identify other finds, I discussed recipes and mushroom preservation with several other veterans. One described a recipe for chanterelles with apricots. Another promised to mail me her favorite recipe for chanterelles with pineapple and shrimp and showed me her unique mobile solar mushroom dehydrator. The back window of her car was spread with trays of chopped chanterelles drying in the magnified—and free—heat of the August sun.

By noon most people were headed off to do what most Northwoods residents and visitors do on beautiful

August Saturdays. I bet some fish were caught, some sunscreen was spread, and some relaxing on decks, docks, and pontoons took place. But I bet most of the foray-goers also made a point to shock a few acquaintances with their new-found knowledge. And hopefully a few of them did what I did after my first experience and went shopping for that personal mushroom basket to flash around on the next foray.

Interested in finding out more or attending a foray? Contact the Paul Bunyan Mushroom Club via their website at pbmushroom.org.

Down at the Dock

To skinny-dip or not to skinny-dip? That was the question facing me as I stood on the dock at 5 o'clock on a Sunday morning. I had walked down the hill with a bucket and a bottle of shampoo, looking to freshen up my hair a bit before heading out on a weeklong vacation. The lake invited me to do more.

The glow of a slow sunrise was commencing through the forest, gently starting to warm a summer day. Wisps of morning lake fog were rising from the warm water, swirling and dancing like fairies on the mirror-calm surface. Sunfish smacked bugs in the lily pads while a heron stalked frogs in the shallows and a brood of half-grown wood ducks foraged in the rushes. Not another human was in sight.

A quick lake water shampoo in my bucket was all that was planned. Now I was wishing for a swimsuit and the luxury of a dive into the cool water. This lack of foresight left three choices. Trudging back up the hill and digging the swimsuit out of the travel bag buried in the back of the truck seemed like a waste of time and energy. Likewise, jumping in partially clothed would be a waste of the limited supply of clean clothes packed for vacation. A quick, discreet skinny-dip while the neighbors snoozed was an inviting third option.

The uneven shoreline of Crooked Lake shields the dock from all but one other cabin. The inhabitants of that cabin are out-of-staters that don't spend much time in these parts and are pretty much unknown to me.

But as fate would have it, they were hanging around this weekend. If any of them happened to be awake for an early cup of coffee, I'm pretty sure the sight of me streaking down my dock might be a bit disturbing.

I'm not the shy type, but I have no desire to get on the local list of people with disturbing habits. Like the neighbor that target-shoots from his deck way too often and the one with the ATV that has its mufflers removed. Or the guy on the south side of the lake that throws loud, late parties without ever inviting us neighbors on the north side of the lake.

It's no secret that some of the neighbors do already question a few of my habits. I'm the one that awakens them before sunrise on October mornings, blasting away at waterfowl from the islands. I'm also the one who inherited the home-made cannon and booms it out across the lake to loudly announce the New Year, the Fourth of July, or any other holiday worthy of an echoing cannon blast. Some of them even question why I use deer carcasses left over from hunting season butchering to feed birds in the winter. This one may seem really weird, but the birds flock to the frozen meat scraps and it doesn't seem to bother other deer. They still eat the new trees planted to replace the trees they already ate, oblivious to remains of their unlucky brethren hanging in the trees above.

But while I may have some "questionable" habits, I don't think the neighbors have yet labeled me as "disturbing." Skinny-dipping in broad morning light might just do that. It might even rate a call to the local authorities and an embarrassing note in the Sheriff's report in the local paper—"Caller reported man swimming naked off dock on north side of Crooked Lake." Even if I was long gone by the time it was investigated, some nosy person could do some digging and trace it back to me.

I was nearing a decision, thinking about erring on the side of caution, when I remembered that the neighbors in question were no angels themselves. They're the ones with the big loud Jet Ski. I always know, as do the loons and the otters, when they are back for a visit. That infernal machine does doughnuts in the bay all afternoon, disturbing the lake and other inhabitants alike.

So, there's the rub. Do I risk being labeled a "disturber" over a quick skinny-dip? Or waste more time worrying while sun brightens the morning and enhances the odds of being caught?

I refuse to incriminate myself and describe what may have happened next. Sometimes a writer needs to leave out the details and let the reader imagine the possible, gruesome, disturbing details. Besides, if a man does skinny-dip at 5 in the morning, and no one sees him, did he really skinny-dip at all?

Inconvenient Truths

Caution, the following discussion may contain statements disturbing to those who care not to believe that spouses, children, friends, or acquaintances can partake in crude, disgusting behaviors. And it may play into the hands of those that believe that people who live and/or recreate in the North Country are not as refined as city folk. However, it's time we talked about two related subjects and faced up to the truth—as disturbing as it may be.

Let's accept the fact that bathrooms are not always convenient and well-placed in rural settings such as remote cabins and farms. This means that people, particularly men, who visit, inhabit, or otherwise hang out in peaceful, private settings may take matters into their own hands and do what comes naturally. Some even take it a step further. Ask a cross section of men what drove them to purchasing a place in the country or drew them to a particular remote property and the answer might be surprising, even shocking to some. A certain portion of the sample is going to say—"I wanted a place where I could take a leak off the deck without someone calling the cops."

Now let's make it clear that I am not a fan of this type of behavior at my rustic little cabin, even though there's nobody to call the cops and the evidence would be long gone by the time they got there. But I understand the underlying philosophy and general train of thought behind the statement. Most of these guys don't really mean it in a literal sense.

There is something to be said for having the ability or the opportunity to mark your territory in broad daylight without the worry of offending a neighbor or making a nuisance walk to the bathroom or outhouse— even if you choose not to exercise that right.

Then let's get past that fact and move on to the related subject of nudity. I'm not saying I'm ready to join the local nudist colony (if there is one), or start one myself. But it is nice to be able to walk to the clothesline, strip off a wet swimsuit and dry off naturally while walking back to the deck in nothing but sandals. I might even enjoy a beer or two in a comfortable chair before looking for a pair of shorts.

Granted there are risks. The sense of remote privacy does lend itself to embarrassing moments, some of which are just plain unfortunate circumstances. Let's call them "random acts of embarrassment." Take one acquaintance of mine. One morning he stepped out of his bedroom onto the deck without wearing pajamas. Maybe he was out to answer the call of nature. Maybe not. In any case, he heard a strange hissing noise from above, followed by laughter. He looked up to find a hot air balloon full of strangers making a slow, low pass over his home. The occupants were amused. He wasn't and has to worry about starring in a viral Internet video.

This example may be unusual in that it involved an aerial intrusion and strangers. My research has shown that the biggest risk is friends and neighbors that show up unannounced, just to see what's up. As an example, another friend, who shall remain nameless to protect his dignity, related this story to me. "There I was, working in the garden, pulling weeds, just trying to get a little sun. Then that dang neighbor (who shall also remain nameless) pulls up. And for once he wasn't driving that noisy old truck. He had his wife's car and I never heard him coming. At least I had my underwear on. But trust me, me in a tiny pair of underwear is something none of us wants to see, even me."

So get real and face up to the truth, as inconvenient as it may be. Things just happen naturally out here in the country. A man may take a break from splitting wood and spend a moment watering the flowers while he is at it. Even I have been known to let the dog out for her morning bathroom break and watch her from the deck with nothing but the radio on. Also remember that like the friends above, most of us do have a sense of modesty and would prefer not to be caught in compromising, embarrassing situations. We realize it most likely is going to be something that can't be unseen.

I'd like to hope that these possibilities don't stop you from being friendly. Feel free to drop in at the cabin anytime and have a beer on the deck while filling me in on the latest fishing hotspot, big buck sighting, or stories about the neighbors. But it might be best to drive an old truck with a bad exhaust, pause at the top of the driveway, and beep the horn before pulling in. Just in case.

Things You Don't Want to Hear at Deer Camp

"Deer Camp." To hunters and non-hunters alike, this term conjures up a picture of an old run-down shack deep in the forest with a woodstove for heat, an outhouse for accommodations, and an entirely male crowd. These guys hang out, drink bad booze, eat fatty foods, belch, smoke stinky cigars, play poker and do everything but hunt deer. The classic deer hunting songs "The Second Week of Deer Camp" (Da Yoopers), "Da Turdy Point Buck" (Bananas At Large), and the corresponding YouTube videos have helped perpetuate this image. And it's not all wrong. Those places still exist and I'm willing to bet that the saying "What happens at Deer Camp, stays at Deer Camp," was around long before Las Vegas turned into a party town.

The Deer Camp where I hang out come November does have some distinct differences from these. Perhaps the main one is the dwelling itself. No run-down log cabin or breezy canvas tent for us. "The Shack" is a low slung cottage-style farmhouse with new vinyl siding, electric heat, a kitchen full of appliances and, perhaps most notable, hot and cold running water and a full service bathroom.

Lest I paint too idyllic a picture, it does have flaws. One that immediately comes to mind is the low ceiling in the upstairs loft. It's roughly five feet high because the original owners were typical uber-frugal Scandinavian farmers who wouldn't spring for the extra-length, extra-cost rafters which would have provided adequate headroom. That means us modern day six-foot-tall deer hunters smack our heads at least once a season on those low and extremely solid rafters.

I've been a part of this get-together for over thirty consecutive years—dang near half my life. It started out as five guys occupying the vacant farmhouse owned by one member's father and uncle. There have been some changes since then. However, three of the five originals, their sons, and a new member or two still show up every November thanks to our gracious hosts and perhaps our relatively good manners. I have to qualify "good" here because there have been a few incidents we wish hadn't happened. There's that bullet hole in the front door for one thing, left there unrepaired as a reminder of an accident that fortunately left no person injured. Trust me, one thing I never want to hear at Deer Camp again is, "I think I just shot the house."

With that infamous phrase in mind, I've compiled a list of the top ten less serious things you don't want to hear at Deer Camp. Some are self-explanatory, some will test your imagination. Also keep in mind that whenever you get six or seven or eight males of the species together in tight quarters for days on end, things are bound to be said and happen that can be taken out of context.

Number 10—"Your wife called—she said something about the furnace at home not working."

Number 9—"It must have got real cold last night —all the beer is frozen solid."

Number 8—"Supper's on me tonight! I found a couple three-year-old venison roasts in the bottom of the freezer and made a big pot of chili."

Number 7—"I always wear long-sleeved T-shirts.

I just cut off a sleeve if I run low on toilet paper out in the woods."

Number 6—"Can you reach the smoke detector? I burned the jalapenos again."

Number 5—"I think these underwear belonged to my grandpa."

Number 4—"Anybody know why there's a dead beaver in the beer fridge?"

Number 3—"Move your butt away from my sandwich, please!"

Number 2—"Stay out of the kitchen. Steve's wearing his thong again."

On second thought, maybe I should quit right here. Now that I think about it, even at our tame place, maybe most of what is said at Deer Camp, should stay at Deer Camp.

The Guessing Game

It's not likely that many people consider deer hunting a spectator sport. However, this opening day of Minnesota deer season finds me sitting on the sidelines of the big event, watching a spread of duck decoys on the pond near the farmhouse. After arriving from a week of deer hunting in Montana, I've decided to let the others have the stands and to try to scratch my duck hunting itch. Still, it's hard to not be wondering and guessing about what's going on in the woods and fields around me.

Once the sun comes up, I will be able to see a couple members of our hunting party. Pete, Munson's oldest son, should be hunkered down on the woodpile at the Funnel, directly west of me. Any deer heading north or south have to funnel between the lake and floating bog, and right past him, to get to the woods. Munson's orange-clad head might be visible to the southwest as he peers out of the Freeway Stand and into the woods surrounding it on three sides. I won't be able to see what my son Steve is up to north along the woods in the Old Man Stand. Likewise hunting partner Darrell is way back in the woods and out of sight in the Oak Lake Stand.

Dave left the shack a few minutes ago and wheeled his old Ford truck south down the township road to his property. I can picture my oldest son Andy riding shotgun with him and anxious to get into the woods now that first light is starting to show. As he already knows, when you hunt with Dave, sometimes things get a little late.

In between him and us are Morris and his son Luther. They were probably out in their stands along the power line well before light, hoping to spot unsuspecting deer leaving the big alfalfa field. To the east are Ken and his daughters, and the usual freeloaders that come with having daughters. Then of course there's Lee, his official sidekick. They have tree fort stands with windows and propane heaters overlooking managed food plots. That's not what I call hunting but then maybe I'm just jealous. This unheated made-from-scratch duck blind is getting a little chilly as the twenty degree sunrise starts. Ken has his lady friend tagging along this morning on her first deer hunt. I wonder how that's going.

Once the action starts, this will be more like listening to a ball game on a bad radio than watching on a widescreen TV. I might get a glimpse of the action at the Funnel but more likely it will be a listening game. A single mild crack of the 6.5mm Husqvarna rifle in Steve's hands likely means a dead deer. Guessing at the size and type of deer will be a real gamble. Steve doesn't often miss and is due back home tomorrow. He won't be fussy when a deer shows. Likewise, the boom of the .30-06 in Munson's hands usually means a dead deer. This year he's shooting some fancy silver-pointed vampire-killer premium bullets. Quite a change from his usual homemade round-nose handloads. The somewhat lighter crack of Darrell's 270 or the other .30-06 in Pete's hands could mean anything. These guys are the most inexperienced and still suspect—at least that's what we tell them.

Speaking of Dave, a truck just drove fast back

up the road. I can't see anything yet but it's soon obvious that Dave must have forgotten something. The truck pulls into the driveway, stops in front of the house, and the house's screen door slams. I don't have to wonder long about what he forgot. The bathroom light in the farmhouse comes on and solves that mystery. I bet Andy is shaking his head and wondering about hunting with us older men and our little quirks.

The first half-hour is quiet for an opening day of Minnesota. The deer appear to be laying low. Ditto for the ducks. Several high-flying flocks of divers wing by high overhead. Not a single one shows an interest in the decoys. My attention is starting to drift just about the time a shot booms out from the woods. I try to zero in and pick the source—most likely Darrell. Then suddenly Munson breaks the stillness with a louder, no-doubt shot from the Freeway. For the next several minutes the woods echo with shots as it seems he and Darrell are in a shooting match. The heavy, close .30-06 booms, the farther 270 answers back. A herd of deer moving back and forth along the swamp between the stands? One lone confused deer looking for a way out of the woods? Munson disappears from his stand. One deer down? Five deer down?

Action seems to pick up all around. A burst of gunfire to the distant south probably means another group of hunters jumped a deer on a drive. In between are several single shots from a big gun. Dave and the 45/70? Andy and the Ruger 44 magnum? Ken's crew to the east adds a few shots to the mix. One series sounds like his daughter Sarah's 243 cracking. But I could be wrong. She doesn't often have to shoot more than once. Silence reigns to the north where Steve is looking

over the wooded fence line. That's usually a sure spot
on opening morning. I wonder what's going on there. Is
he fast asleep in the safe comfortable box stand? It
wouldn't be the first time.

   After an hour of the guessing, things start to
come together. I spot Munson walking out from the
Freeway down the narrow peninsula between the bog and
my duck pond. It looks like his son Peter has moved
from the Funnel and into the Freeway. Munson strolls
out into an opening on the lakeshore, the unhurried
walk of a contented hunter who has had success. He
stops, waves to me, and points to the heavy plastic
bag he is carrying in the other hand.

   I trade my duck hunting camo for a hunter-orange
deer hunting parka, collect my stuff, and push the
canoe into the water. Munson is a camp cook
extraordinaire and doesn't like to waste meat. One of
his specialties is fresh deer heart and liver, coated
in seasoned flour and fried in bacon grease with
plenty of onions. I may not know what's going on with
the other guys, but I'm pretty certain Munson and I
are having brunch together.

Black Powder in
the Bunyan

I pause on the slippery ice, feeling the cold bite of the wind sweeping across the barren expanse of the lake. The dim glow of a December sunrise is struggling to cut through the five-below air. Muffled by my icicle-crusted mustache and itchy wool facemask, I whisper advice to my son Andy: "Head up over the ridge at the birch clump, then sneak into the pines by the beaver pond. I'll walk down the bay and come in from the south."

Suddenly the ice booms and ripples beneath us, shocking us with a brief, primeval moment of fear and panic. We recover and grin sheepishly at each other, both of us slightly unnerved. The lake's groaning, shifting, and rumbling had caught us off guard with a Minnesota-style earthquake.

Andy checks his gun one last time and heads up the steep bank into the forest, his hunter-orange coat glowing in the morning murk. Behind him to the west, last night's full moon is hovering above the trees, fading away with the dawn. I linger to take in the scene and wait for just a bit more light.

Andy and I are using the cabin on the edge of the Paul Bunyan State Forest, or The Bunyan as it's locally known, as a home base for the late muzzleloader deer season. The frozen lake makes a convenient winter expressway into remote parts of the forest. The ice beneath me, despite its disconcerting groans, is a solid eight inches thick. In a normal year, it would be covered with boot-deep snow. This year there's just a thin, white ring of snow clinging to the rim of the lake and a light frosting in the forest. Only a straight-walking fox and a hip-hopping squirrel have disturbed the pristine whiteness with their footprints.

I hike down the bay and leave the open ice for the welcoming shelter of the forest. Andy is somewhere north of me, probably half a mile away, quietly moving through the woods. While he's a veteran of nearly twenty November firearm deer seasons, this is the first year he has tried the late muzzleloader season. Like the vast majority of contemporary muzzleloader hunters, he's carrying a high-tech, plastic-stocked rifle. The blued steel barrel is topped with bright fiber-optic sights and loaded with modern gun powder and plastic-coated bullets. Although the barrel is loaded one shot at a time with a ramrod, there's no doubt that his muzzleloader is a modern-day weapon.

I've chosen to give the deer a little more of an advantage. The gun in my hands could be a well-preserved antique, one that Kit Carson, Jim Bridger, or some less famous mountain man would have carried more than 150 years ago. Unlike Andy's generic store-bought gun, mine was built from a kit. I sanded the walnut stock smooth, layered on multiple coats of traditional oil finish, and used an acid solution to rust the barrel and other metal to a rich, dark brown. As a final personal touch, I inlaid ovals of German silver into the stock. It's a solid, functional replica of a piece of American history.

I'm hoping one of the wary deer that survived last month's regular hunting season will make a mistake and let me get close, real close. The heavy .54 caliber rifle is loaded with historically correct materials, straight from the mid-1800s—coarse grains of loose black powder, a cast-lead bullet lubricated with natural mink oil, and a tiny copper percussion cap.

If I do find a deer, if it is within fifty yards, and if it is standing still, I'll have to cock the hammer, focus my aging eyes over unlit sights, and pull the trigger to make the hammer smack the percussion cap. If I faithfully followed the loading ritual practiced for more than twenty-five years, a spark from the percussion cap will ignite the powder with a roaring boom and a thick cloud of reeking sulfurous smoke. If I miss, there will be no second chance.

Without snow, the leaves covering the old logging road are brittle and crunchy. I tiptoe down the trail, doing my best imitation of a deer with dainty, pointy hoofs. I wonder what those old leather- and fur-clad mountain men would think of me. The gun wouldn't draw a second glance. However, they might laugh out loud at my bright orange and black "camouflage" coat.

If there were more snow, I'd pick a fresh set of tracks and follow them, sneaking along through pine groves and over hardwood ridges, hoping to see the deer before it sees me. Without the snow, I'm searching for a brownish-gray deer in a brownish-gray forest, relying on experience to predict where my quarry might be. With or without snow, this method of hunting is as old as these hills and one with a personal, historic connection. My grandfather and uncle hunted this way in the Bunyan, more than seventy years ago. The antlers of a ten-point buck Grandpa took in 1939 are hanging in my cabin.

Hunting methods have changed since the passing of the old fur trappers and, more recently, my grandpa. Freely roaming the woods during the November firearm season is uncommon these days. The early-season hunters erect tree stands, hunker down with telescope-sighted rifles, and let the deer come to them. Other hunters respect the unmarked boundaries around these stands and stay away.

Today all these lonely platforms of weathered boards, rusted metal ladders, and faded camouflage seats, so coveted and protected only a month ago, are eerily vacant. Few other hunters seem willing to brave the cold and the snowless woods this time of year, even with their modern muzzleloaders.

Late in the morning, I pick a sheltered ridge overlooking the lake and sit down to enjoy the Northwoods ambiance and a hot cup of coffee. From this vantage point, the cold, dense air carries the sound of other lakes and ponds making ice—twanging, pinging, and thumping. A fluffy black-capped chickadee checks me out from a nearby branch before fluttering down onto my gun barrel and perching near the front sight. Next comes a hyperactive squirrel, with rusty-red fur that seems dyed to match the dried pine needles on the forest floor. It challenges me with feisty chatter and then tramps around, sounding exactly like a trophy buck.

Amid all these distractions, I do sometimes find deer. Or sometimes they find me. Two years ago, not far from here, I was enjoying my coffee in a grove of snow-covered pines. Suddenly, shadows flickered in front of me. Two big, horizontal shapes moved purposefully through sunlit gaps between the pines.

I had to sacrifice my coffee that morning: It spilled warmly over my lap as I brought the gun up. The lead deer stepped behind a thicket of brush barely ten yards away. I tried to muffle the loud click of the hammer as it was thumbed back. But something gave me away. Both deer stopped and instantly seemed to disappear, so near, but so perfectly camouflaged. Much goes through your mind in heart-pounding situations like that, with only one shot and no margin for error. Nagging doubts about the primitive gun. Worries about a whiff of scent carried on a stray breeze. Take the closer deer, obviously a doe? Or take a chance, wait for the second deer, maybe a buck?

The tense standoff ended when the doe sidestepped from cover and froze, head down, looking directly at me. No more time to think. The big gun boomed out, completely obscuring the scene with a cloud of white-gray smoke. When the air cleared and the echoes subsided, the second deer was gone. The first remained, down and unmoving in the pine needles and snow. The gun had humanely done its job, despite the inhospitable weather and its two-hundred-year-old design.

My luck does not repeat this morning. I finish my coffee uninterrupted while the chickadees and squirrels entertain and the lake provides background music. The cold starts to seep through my high-tech clothes and the comforts of my cozy cabin beckon me from nearly a mile away. The cabin will still be warm, even if the oak in the woodstove has burned down to a few glowing embers. Kaliber, the elderly Labrador Retriever Andy and I left behind, will be pouting in her favorite chair, unhappy she was not invited to tag along.

I step onto the windswept ice and start the long hike back to the cabin, eager to stoke the stove, thaw my mustache, and compare notes with Andy. It's shaping up to be a difficult hunt. Zero snow, zero deer, and the temperature is even less than zero. But the ice is rumbling beneath me, the gun is balanced comfortably in my arms, and there's not another person in sight. I'm feeling alive and free in the Bunyan.

Don't Tell My Wife

I recently returned from a deer hunting road trip to Montana and found the house empty. My wife and her sister had decided to take the dogs and head off on a road trip of their own. I was hankering for companionship, conversation, and doggie kisses after spending a week in the wilds alone. However, this meant I had the garage, the basement, the rest of the house, and the washer and dryer all to myself for two days. I was a very lucky man.

Let's start with the unpacking part. There was no rush to unload the truck, unpack, clean, repack and reorganize immediately given the not-so-spacious confines of our little home. I was able to spread my gear and clothing, or all my "junk" as Marcie would have called it, far and wide across the garage, basement, and upstairs. I took two days to unpack, even found a knife and the extra mantles for my gas lantern that had been given up for lost since the year before.

Most important in the unpacking department was that I didn't have to struggle to explain why so many clothes had gone with me to Montana—and why so few of them were coming back used. She might have even noticed the lack of changes of underwear and the fact I was still wearing the pair of camouflage jeans that I left in. There are explanations for all of this, sort of. But it's just as well I didn't have to go into them.

Cutting up and wrapping the deer I brought home was also much more relaxed and stress-free. Let's face it, in spite of the fact that I am a trained professional when it comes to food preparation and sanitation, home butchering can get messy, maybe even gruesome. The coolers and the sink are bound to look just a little like a crime scene. Lucky for me, there was time to clean up and hide the evidence. I even checked the sink strainer to make sure no surprises were hiding there.

I did miss Marcie's skills in the meat-wrapping department. My meat packages are wrapped like my Christmas presents: lots of tape and extra paper hanging out here and there from odd corners. The writing on the packages and the code words and abbreviations used often need interpretation afterwards. I will also note the dogs were missed during this exercise. Whether it's a weekend at the cabin with lots of food and friends, or a solitary couple of days butchering deer at home, the floor is always a little cleaner with them hanging around looking for targets of opportunity.

I think I did a good job of making the place look respectable. I'm even pretty proud of passing on one temptation. Ever heard of a "game bag"? They're large heavy-duty open-weave cotton bags used to transport the meat from game animals back to camp and/or home. Good ones cost about five bucks apiece. While unpacking, I noticed a claim on the label of a bag. *May be washed and reused,* it said. Well, why not? I had four well-used ones that had each held twenty pounds of raw meat for four days. Who wouldn't want to save twenty dollars?

I hauled the grisly bags down to the laundry room and stood over the washing machine contemplating which settings to use. I am no novice to the machine but I didn't see a "get rid of the bloody evidence" wash cycle. Other questions soon came to mind. Would hot water shrink and spoil the bags while performing needed sanitary functions? What questionable evidence might show up in the dryer's lint filter should I forget to clean that? Would Marcie see the "clean" game bags and wonder how they got that way?

I came to the realization even a mafia hit man would not be able to hide all the evidence from what I was considering. I hauled the bags out to the garbage can and tossed them in. I wasn't feeling that lucky.

Six Men in a Boat

The fish smacked Dale's crawfish-colored lure just as the boat turned toward the windswept island. With the wind pushing hard towards the wave-battered rocks lining the shore, he struggled to control the tiller with one hand and a bent fishing rod with the other.

"Big fish," he yelled over the noise of the wind and motor. "REALLY big fish!"

I kept an eye on the rocks while readying the net and balancing near the rail of the rocking boat. I didn't know yet that two first-time experiences were coming up in the next moments. Dale fought the fish, taking line, losing line, the wind and waves aiding the fish and complicating the battle. Things got real interesting when the fish showed itself in the foaming tea-stained water. Attached to the end of the line with an orange crankbait clamped in its jaws was exactly what we had come here for: a huge old battle-scarred walleye.

I leaned way out and slid the net under the first thirty-plus-inch walleye I have ever netted. Then came the second first. A wave rocked the boat with me hanging out over the water, extended to the max with a heavy fish flopping in the net. Gravity and physics took control. I rolled head first out of the boat into the cold waters of Ontario's Lake of the Woods.

Speaking of firsts, this was my first fishing trip to Canada. Dale, my brother-in-law and a fishing tackle salesman, called months ago in the dead of a Minnesota winter. "We're adding two guys to our Lake of the Woods houseboat trip," he said. "Are you in?"

An offer like that doesn't come often enough—a chance to share an adventure with four experienced fishermen to their remote hotspot. We would meet at Sioux Narrows, Ontario, load equipment and supplies onto a rented houseboat, tie three fishing boats behind, and head twenty-five miles out into the islands, channels, and bays that make up the wild northeast corner of Lake of the Woods. I took a chance and committed without even asking my wife.

Every expedition needs a leader, someone to take charge. In this case, Rich, the grizzled veteran of nearly thirty of these trips, sent out a supply list, assigned meals, and kept in touch with the houseboat company. Dale offered advice on equipment and kept me interested with tales of previous trips and fishing hotspots with code names not found on lake maps: Stumpfire Island, Blue Camel Point, Dick's Point, and Mosquito Island.

We converged on Sioux Narrows on a Friday afternoon in mid-June. The forty-foot houseboat reserved for this trip had been rented the week before and wouldn't be gassed up and cleaned until the next morning. This left time to pick up a few last-minute supplies and hang out at a historic fishing lodge for the night. The big adventure got started Saturday morning, loading what seemed like an entire grocery store worth of food and beverages onto the boat.

Here's one of the beauties of a houseboat. No freeze-dried food for us. The pantry, refrigerator, and freezer were well stocked with everything from eggs to salad. And yes, let's just say there was plenty of bacon on board. With that accomplished, we cast off and started the twenty-five mile voyage, plodding along at five miles an hour while winding through a maze of islands and channels marked at random intervals by buoys.

This part of Lake of the Woods has a real Up North Canadian wilderness look. Rocky islands shove up out of the lake in random sizes and locations, varying from one-rock/one-pine tree outcrops to hundreds of acres of forest-covered wilderness. Stumpfire Island, our home anchorage for the next six days, proved to be a two-acre hunk of rock and pine trees sheltered by other larger islands. Beaching on the narrow strip of gravel shoreline was a high stress maneuver with the bulky houseboat. Two crew members untied fishing boats and landed on the island as a shore crew. Two more climbed to the top deck and tossed ashore heavy lines to tie off around big pine trees. Thus solidly secured to the island, it was time to fish.

Dale and I hopped into his fishing boat and headed to a spot a mile from our island. The GPS was loaded with the latest updated lake bottom contours and showed a rocky point tapering down 200 yards out into the lake and ending on a thirty-foot flat. Twelve dozen nightcrawlers came along for the trip to Canada. Dale dropped one of these over the side, rigged on a spinner with a two-hook harness. I went with a half-ounce jig tipped with a short piece of crawler. A fat eighteen-inch walleye hit the spinner rig Dale offered and the bite was on. Two more fell for the spinner and crawler before my jig got action—all nice fifteen- to eighteen-inch fish. This was Canadian fishing—even I could catch them!

The next five days settled into a rhythm of sleep, eat, fish, eat, campfire, and sleep again. I can't vouch for how good the fishing is at sunrise on Lake of the Woods. That's because sunrise is around 5 a.m. and nobody was up at sunrise. However, it stays light in this part of the world until past 11 o'clock—there's plenty of time to fish. We slept in every morning and had a huge breakfast cooked by the chef of the day. I'm happy to say our bacon supply held up well.

With breakfast under our belts, we hit the water, stayed out until midafternoon, returned for a light lunch, then fished hard until returning for supper. This meal featured the main stay of our catch—white-fleshed walleye fillets fresh from the lake. Then it was time to retire to the fire ring on the island, watching the sun fade and the stars break out, while telling fish tales old and new to the accompaniment of loons yodeling and eagles shrieking in a nest on the next island.

The fishing followed patterns, too. We found hungry walleyes in two distinct types of structure. There were deep fish scattered along twenty-foot flats off points and islands. My early attempts at jig fishing proved to be costly in these areas due to the rocky crevices ready to swallow a jig and keep it. I switched to Dale's favorite crawler harness and spinner combination fished behind a half-ounce no-snag sinker. Just feel for bottom, raise up about a foot and let the walleyes zero in on the crawler trailing behind the thumping spinner. This technique was deadly for eating-size walleyes in the fifteen- to eighteen-inch range.

The spinner and crawler combos also served up a few surprises—like the occasional small mouth bass and jumbo perch. But one fish hit in thirty feet of water and headed the opposite direction in a screaming long distance run. My medium-weight rod and eight-pound test monofilament line were badly over-matched. A big northern pike somersaulted out of the water a long ways from the boat, splashed back in, and went deep for a prolonged fight. I'd work him close. He'd poke his alligator-like head out of the water, see the boat, and dive down on another long run. In the end he tired on the surface and eyed me with an evil look as he was eased towards the boat and netted. Thirty-nine inches of muscular, pure mean, toothy, green and white fish was released back into the depths after the photo opportunity.

More fun than the bottom-bouncing was trolling crayfish-patterned orange crankbaits along rocky, windy shorelines in ten to fifteen feet of water. Moving along at two to three miles an hour, the lure would stop with a thump and the rod would bend over. Sometimes it was just a rock on the other end. But many times what initially felt like a rock, wasn't a rock. I'd tell Dale to circle back only to have the "rock" suddenly shake its head and head the opposite direction full of fight.

The biggest walleyes came this way and more of those surprises. Midway through the week my crankbait found one of those "rock fish." Light mono line and rod were put to the test again as a mystery fish took long runs in shallow water between two islands, circling the boat with me hanging on and scrambling over tackle and seats to keep up. Ten minutes later a thirty-six-inch muskie was in the net. That isn't huge for a muskie. But as a non-muskie fisherman, it ranked as my best ever and put up a memorable battle on the light tackle. Feisty smallmouth bass and northern pike liked these tactics too. The bass were as round as footballs. The northern pike and muskies were fat and heavy with massive girths—not the long snaky types often found farther south.

These bonus fish aside, big walleyes were the main attraction. Rich managed to land a thirty-one-incher early in the trip. The weight would have been around twelve pounds or more if the catch-and-release charts are right. I managed a twenty-seven-incher as my personal best—caught on a crankbait trolled along a rocky shore on the last day of the trip. The other guys all caught similar fish. In between, we each boated about twenty-five walleyes a day, with perch, sauger, smallmouth bass, northern pike, and the occasional muskie. We had no trouble eating walleyes every day while stashing a few seventeen- to eighteen-inch fish and some bonus perch for the trip home.

And that big walleye I was netting while rolling out of the boat? I was able to pass the net handle off to Dale on the way into the water. Yes, I was wearing a life jacket. And a non-waterproof camera. Dale managed to pull the fish into the boat and steer away from the rocks while helping me roll back onboard, baptized in the cold water of Lake of the Woods. It was his biggest walleye, thirty and a half inches, fat, and scarred by a long hard life.

Dale chose to release that whopper to fight again another day. It's too bad he didn't get a good picture of it since our only camera was baptized with me and didn't survive. He will have to make do with the memory, one heck of a story, and hope that his net man can stay dry next year.

Escape From
Stumpfire Island

My first trip to Canada's Lake of the Woods was an experience not soon forgotten and one that begged for a return engagement. I got to spend a week of quality male-bonding time with five other outdoorsmen. I caught both the biggest northern pike and muskie of my long fishing life—and some of the biggest walleyes. The scenery was grand as were the nightly campfires overlooking a near-wilderness setting with loons and eagles calling and the northern lights glowing on the horizon. Even falling overboard into the icy waters was only a minor issue and one that left me, and the other guys, with a great tale to be retold around the campfire for many more trips to come.

Tagging along with these guys had definite benefits—like three high-tech fishing boats and the knowledge that comes from fishing the same area for thirty years. I'm used to being the guide and boat driver on most fishing excursions. On this trip, all I had to do was sit back, admire the scenery, watch for wildlife, and catch walleyes while Dale drove his boat and guided. The only downside, and I hesitate to even call it that, was the mornings. I was restless, looking for adventure, and ready to hit the water at sunrise, even after the late nights at the campfire. The other guys were on vacation and chose to sleep in. I can't blame them. The bacon still tasted great when served as a late brunch and the fish didn't care what time of the day they attacked our bait.

I hatched a plan for the next year. Bringing my own boat made no sense. It would just add cost and hassle. Taking Dale's boat out alone was risky. The rocky islands in this part of the world are unpredictable. One might rise up a hundred feet from the lake, covered with pine trees and wildlife. Another lurks just below the surface, harboring fish and a desire to rip the lower unit from any nearby outboard motor. After seeing more than a few of these shallow hazards, many marked with shiny streaks of aluminum from the motors and bottoms of other unsuspecting boaters, I had no desire to be out on my own with another person's expensive boat. This need for independence seemed like the perfect excuse to buy a fishing kayak.

So I started doing research and looking for deals on kayaks as soon as we got back. But before I could invest, the motor blew on my main fishing boat and with it went the better part of my kayak-buying budget. My plan was sunk—until a big home improvement store advertised a truckload sale on entry level kayaks, complete with free paddle. One of these would have to do. I won't tell you how little this addition to my fleet cost. I'm too embarrassed—really.

There wasn't much time for the trial and error method of converting this basic kayak into a specialized fishing machine, so I consulted the Internet kayak fishing gurus. That's when I stumbled across video clips of guys creating all manner of rod holders and other accessories from plain old white plastic pipe. I made another visit to that home improvement store, this time to the plumbing section. Ten dollars worth of pipe and fittings later and my new kayak was sporting a double rod holder with a built-in cup holder.

We tucked the kayak into Dale's boat for the next trip, imported it to Canada, and stashed it on the roof of the houseboat for the cruise to Stumpfire Island. This trip was much like the first. We ate bacon at mid to late morning, fished the rest of the day, caught huge numbers and sizes of fish, and wasted away the evenings at the campfire with loons calling and a good drink in hand. Only early mornings were different. While the other guys loudly snored, I escaped the island, stole away in my tangerine-colored plastic yacht, and had the lake to myself.

The small northern pike and bass near the houseboat occupied me for a few mornings and schooled me in kayak fishing. I learned about things like tying the paddle to the kayak so it didn't drift away when I dropped it to fight a fish and how far a small fish could pull me in this light little piece of plastic. On the third morning I got brave. I paddled down the shore of the island and ventured off a rocky point into thirty feet of water. My only competitors were the loons, the eagles, and the pelicans flying and floating past on their own fishing excursions.

A half-ounce jig tipped with a nightcrawler chunk went over the side, found the bottom, and was jigged up and down. Walleye after walleye attacked the jig and towed me in tight circles before surfacing. After a satisfying hour of catching and releasing average-sized fish, I flipped a crankbait behind the kayak and paddle-trolled back towards the houseboat with bacon on my mind.

I was in sight of the houseboat, rounding the corner of the island when the rod whipped back and the kayak spun around. For a minute it seemed like Moby Dick had smacked the lure and was about to tow me off to sea. But the bend of the rod and the drag of the kayak tired the fish. A few minutes later I managed to get it alongside and lifted a fat two-foot-long walleye from the water. After a series of photos that endangered the non-waterproof camera, it was released to fight again.

It wasn't the biggest walleye I caught on the trip. It was the most memorable. I caught it my way, on my own time. At least in the mornings, I was Master of my own destiny—and Captain of my own little ship.

Ice Cold Lakers

I hold the portable GPS out the truck window, following the arrow, plowing through eight inches of snow and minor drifts until the magic machine indicates we had reached "The Spot." The truck skids to a halt on the ice. I hesitate a minute before shutting the engine down, basking in the hot air blowing out of the heater vents. My moment of warm bliss doesn't last long. Oldest son Andy looks at me from the shotgun seat—"Come on—let's do it!" We roll out the truck doors and into fresh, clean, thirty-five degree below zero Northwoods air. The scramble is on—pulling on insulated bibs, thick socks, warm boots, duck hunting parka, and a warm hat. It isn't a matching ensemble when finished but when fishing for lake trout on a frozen lake just south of Canada, functional warmth is going to conquer high fashion every time.

Andy pops the back of the truck open and starts unloading tackle bags, rod cases, portable fish houses, and the all-important gas ice auger—a big three-horsepower beast with a ten-inch blade guaranteed to bore through two feet of ice in less than twenty seconds. The dang thing is also guaranteed to get the swearing started for the day. I flip the switch to "On," push the choke lever to "Full," pump the primer bulb three times, and give the starter a pull. Perhaps a short prayer should have been uttered first. The cord breaks and flies back, smacking me in the face as the starter spring unwinds in the housing. Andy doesn't say much. He pulls the small backup auger out of the truck, fires it up without incident, and starts grinding holes through two feet of ice, thus drowning out the bad words flowing from my way.

Ice fishing for lake trout in the Far North in the dead of winter isn't for the unprepared or the faint of heart. Expect thirty or thirty-five below temperatures. Expect plastic handles to break off as you open a truck door or tailgate. Expect the rock-bottom temperatures to expose all sorts of flaws in high-tech gear including broken zippers on parkas, dead batteries in fish finders, and ice augers that refuse to start. Expect to cuss a lot. Fortunately, also expect to find hard-fighting trout on scenic, isolated lakes studded with rocky islands and surrounded by snow-flocked pines.

Most people think dog sleds, cross-country skis, or snowshoes when picturing ice fishing in extreme northern Minnesota. But for those willing to brave the cold, numerous easier-to-reach lakes have the potential for big trout. Andy and I have repeatedly proven that a dog sled, snowmobile, or ATV isn't essential to enjoy this cold weather fishing. A look at a good map and the usual Internet sources will reveal an endless supply of lakes, more fishing spots than can be explored in a lifetime.

An eight-pound lake trout on six- or eight-pound test and a short ice fishing rod is no wimpy, sluggish walleye. If a red blur shows up on the fish finder's flasher and streaks in for a look, get ready, there might be a long fight ahead. These fish will peel line off a little ice reel until you get real worried. Then they fight all the way back, taking back five feet of line for every ten gained. When the fish nears the hole, expect diving, twisting, whirling, and brief glimpses of copper-colored fins tipped in ivory attached to a chunky gold- and green-speckled body. That's when the heartache and bad words can really flow.

I've done some amateur videos of these struggles. One from a few years ago stands out. A fat green and gold lake trout repeatedly swims through the clear water past the hole, the line tangled behind front fins from the struggle. Andy tries to guide its head up the hole, fighting the weight of the fish and the weird physics from the angle of the tangled line. The air in the portable fish house turns white from the icy air rolling in the open door, then blue from the adult language from two frustrated fishermen. The camera man, yours truly, reaches into the frame and down the hole to assist. For a moment there's hope. Then the lure pulls free, pops out of the hole, the fish is gone, and all other sound is drowned out by words my wife and Andy's mother would not want to hear.

Fortunately, it's not always like that. After all, we keep coming back in spite of the troubles. I complete the repairs to the recoil starter, made easier by experience and harder by the cold, start the big auger and punch holes across the rocky structure of a sunken island, staggered over twenty-five to sixty feet of water. Since the lake we are on is not a designated trout lake, two lines and live bait are legal. Two tip-ups baited with four-inch rainbow minnows are set near the bottom in thirty and forty feet. Andy sets up the big green portable fish house off a steep underwater rock wall in thirty feet and disappears inside with his propane heater. I pop up the small blue portable over a point in forty-five feet and drop an airplane jig covered with a bass tube down the hole into the dark abyss. The heater slowly warms the interior and the flasher whirs a comforting purr.

I'm the first to score. A half-hour into the day, something thumps my lure and a short battle is on. I yell "Fish on!" and work the fish close to the hole. Andy unzips from his house and sprints over, just in time to bury his hand down the hole and grab a nineteen-inch, three-pound lake trout. It's a small fish for this spot but a fat, tasty start to the day.

We fish on, occasionally scraping frost from

fish house windows to check for tip-up flags. An hour later I'm rewarded with the orange flag of a tip-up waving in the breeze. I stumble through the tight zipper door, yelling to alert Andy once I see the tip-up reel spinning wildly. The laker has stripped off fifty yards of line by the time I grab it. This time it's hand-to-hand combat without the benefit of a rod and no reel to store the line. The wet line piles around my feet, freezing into interesting tangles as I gain a few feet then lose a few through my bare, rapidly numbing fingers. Andy swoops in when the fish's head appears in the hole and scoops a chunky twenty-four-inch beauty from the hole.

The rest of the day slowly warms to single digits below. I hole hop, looking for active fish until fingers and toes go numb, then retreat to the warmth of the heater in the fish house. Lunch of grilled chili dogs on the truck tailgate comes and goes. Sunset and the threat of another cold northern night bears down on us. Andy is still fishless, parked over his favorite spot, refusing to admit defeat.

Another badly done video chronicles what happens next. I'm busy packing the truck when he yells from his house. I open the door and hold back the door flap with the camera going, frost boiling out as the cold outside air hits the warm air of the fish house. A wimpy little panfish rod is in Andy's hands, bent much more than the manufacturer ever meant it to be. He glances up for a second—"I was messing around with a crappie jig and a big S.O.B. hit it!"

Many minutes later the video camera shows a beautiful green and gold shape sliding past the hole in the clear water, teasing us. I reach toward the hole with a gaff hook, then pull it back when Andy yells, "Just grab his $%#ing head! GRAB HIS %$&*ING HEAD!"

I wait until the thrashing head reappears in the hole and make my move—grabbing the fish's $%&*ing head behind the gills, hauling a floppy, twisting trout past the camera lens and back out the door into the cold. Andy emerges from the house in his camo bibs, his tongue hanging out like a Labrador Retriever after a tough retrieve. I hand him seven or eight pounds of squirming fish and back off to continue videoing the moment.

I try to say something colorful, manly, and profound for the camera's microphone. It comes out as a mumbled mish-mash that makes no sense. I'm too damn cold to even swear.

Huntin' Car

Imagine for a moment you are driving down a gravel country road. An old green tractor comes by, driving down the opposing lane. On it are two boys that look to be in their early teens. And then it dawns on you. "They're carrying guns on that John Deere!"

Do you wave and drive on? Wonder "What the hell?" Or do you pull over and dial 911 on the cellphone? It may be hard to imagine these days but fifty years ago that would have been me and my friend Jimmy Smith. That tractor was our ticket to freedom—driving many slow miles on weekend afternoons, hunting rabbits, squirrels, pigeons, and the occasional pheasant.

Jimmy Smith had the same problems I did—no driver's license and a desire to hunt anything that moved and was legal. Luckily he lived on a farm a couple miles from town and had access to the old green tractor and the farm gas barrel when he and the tractor weren't doing real work. He would pick me up at the edge of town and we would be off, hunting the woodlots and farm groves dotting the countryside. It was a time and place where two young boys with guns were welcome visitors to most farms. We might even get cookies from the kitchen and a hearty thanks for thinning out the grain-robbing, corn crib-chewing varmints or the hay-fouling barn pigeons.

We soon graduated to other vehicles with more room and speed than the tractor. Mine was a 1963

Rambler Classic hand-me-down, Jimmy's a hot red '63 Impala SS. His had the horse power and female attraction edge. Mine had fold-down seats for overnight excursions and four doors for easy access to equipment. I would argue it was actually the better hunting vehicle. Since then there have been many others—a couple of station wagons, more pickup trucks, and an occasional SUV or two. All were attempts at compromise—trying to find that perfect combination that wouldn't embarrass the family and yet could handle a few passengers, a canoe on the roof, a trailer behind, and dirt, fur, feathers, and dog hair.

But when I look back at all of these, there's one that stands out. My college roommate Rod, a.k.a. Dick, bought it in the fall of 1972. Unlike us other destitute college kids, he had a fast car and some money, and did not mind sharing. However, cruising down northern Minnesota logging trails looking for grouse in a 1970 Chevelle muscle car had numerous problems. So he invested $50 in "Huntin' Car." She (we always referred to her in the feminine gender) was a 1952 four-door Chevy Deluxe (properly pronounced DEEEE-lux) complete with chrome airplane hood ornament.

Huntin' Car was with us for two memorable years, those early college years with no responsibilities (higher grades would have been nice), minor money worries (compared to today anyway), and no wives, kids, or even girlfriends (dang it . . .) to stand in the way of fun. We cruised the back roads and the back, back roads in Huntin' Car, seeking out the best grouse spots and a few good duck ponds. These were the glory years of grouse hunting in Minnesota. They were everywhere and we were there every weekend.

Huntin' Car

Huntin' Car had a rusty green paint job and a huge well-used tan interior. She did not fit the definition of "cherry" that a collector would have looked for. Improvements were added for a customized appearance—bullet holes, shotgun patterns, a purposely caved-in roof for that "rolled over" look, and an accidentally cracked windshield. A trip down Main Street on a Friday night was a sure way to get tourists to stop, stare, and conjure up stereotypes about the local inhabitants.

Those Friday night excursions aside, where she excelled was as Huntin' Car. The straight-six engine and three-on-the-tree manual transmission provided ample power. The weight of all that good old-fashioned Detroit iron supplied traction in mud and snow even with just two-wheel drive. And the big shiny chrome front bumper would make even a rutting bull moose turn tail and run.

There were few places out of our reach. A favorite spot was on the far side of a beaver pond-flooded logging road. No problem for Huntin' Car. Just pour on the power downhill and splash across the flooded road with all hands clutching the grab handles conveniently placed throughout the interior. Speed, mass, and gravity were in our favor. The engine would get wet and die at the top of the hill on the other side, right on the edge of prime hunting grounds. It would dry out during the hunt and would be ready for the reverse trip. Though it might sputter to a stop again on the other side, there were grouse in the woods there too. "You can do that with a Huntin' Car" became our motto, our mantra, as a tree was pushed out of a trail, a pond forded, or the railroad tracks used for a short cut.

But nothing lasts forever and neither did Huntin' Car. Her short adventure-filled career ended at the top of a hill on the highway south of town when her oil plug worked loose and allowed her bodily fluids to drain out onto the tar. She still had the guts, the decency, and the will power to limp into the parking lot of the local tavern before freezing up for good. Twenty-five cent frosty mugs of Hamm's beer toasted memories long into the night and part of the morning.

No pictures of Huntin' Car survive, which is just as well. We have all matured at least a bit since those days. Yet her ignition key still hangs on my key chain over forty years later as a remembrance of those happy days with no worries and many grouse flushing down logging roads ablaze with October color. The experiments with trucks, SUVs, and maybe even an old tractor will continue, machines with character and experience to be used as vehicles to more adventures and memories. But it isn't a quest for perfection or for the ultimate hunting vehicle. I've already had that. I had Huntin' Car.

Judgment Day

It was time. Once in a while, a man is forced to face the realities of life, part with one of his most prized possessions, and move on. In this case it was my old green truck. After faithfully serving for more than nine years and accumulating over 192,000 "highway" miles, my slightly used, one-owner, locally owned compact pickup needed replacement.

The tough old truck still looked pretty good and seemed trustworthy. Enough so that I took it on one last trip into the badlands of Montana and lived to tell about it. However, a recent trip to the mechanic revealed the need for $1,000 in updates and repairs. Besides that, something a bit bigger was needed, something that could carry more than two people, a Labrador Retriever, and a fluffy little mutt.

I started by removing the topper. I had a dealership in mind for the trade, a place where a friend of the family worked. Laura advised me to ditch the topper if it didn't improve the overall appearance of the truck. Given that the topper was thirty years old, didn't match the color of the truck, and had plywood replacing one of the windows, that was an easy decision.

It was also obvious, with no advice needed from Laura, that the truck needed a thorough cleanout before making that final trip. Marcie offered to help. We dug in, literally, and filled five bags full of "truck stuff"—manly truck stuff that accumulates under seats, behind seats, in seats, and in the bed of a truck when you are a man, own that same truck for nine years, and actually use it like a truck.

Those who know me will be tempted to ask if I found anything dead in the truck, given my bad habits of hunting and fishing and the odor that emanated from the truck interior on hot summer days. Nope—nothing dead. Unless you count the handful of mallard duck feathers that were floating around in the bed, holdovers from last fall's duck season. There wasn't much spare change either—only thirty-nine cents worth of coins. Not much of a down payment on the new vehicle.

The vehicle trade went down smooth. Laura helped set me up with a shiny white, almost new SUV with all kinds of off-road options that could get me out of lots of trouble or into lots of trouble on the next trip to Montana. Only time will tell how that works out. Now came the hard part, deciding what from those five bags of manly truck stuff was worthy of making the move to the shiny, slightly used, clean SUV.

Some stuff fell into the "no-brainer-toss" category. Stuff that really wasn't needed now or in the future, or was well past its prime. Like the handful of duck feathers and the odd rusted nails, bolts and washers. Likewise, it was time to recycle a bunch of tattered coffee-stained maps, past-expiration-date single-serve ketchup packets, hunting licenses for long past years, and the fishing regulation book from the year the old truck was bought.

In the "no-brainer-save" category was the doggie blanket, still legible road maps for the five states I frequent, and a key ring loaded with about twenty keys that might open something, somewhere, sometime. Then there was the ice scraper (never know when you might need one of those in Minnesota), a box of 12-gauge shotgun shells, a box of 22 rifle shells, a roll of duct tape, and a bunch of zip ties that fit that same category. You never know when you are going to need those either.

Some of the other truck stuff was harder to decide on. Like the pile of assorted tools—pliers, wrenches, screwdrivers, and a heavy duty socket set. They had been a security blanket in the old truck since I had to be ready to fix all kinds of bad things alone in the bad places I go. Were they needed in this barely used SUV with a bumper-to-bumper warranty still intact? And what about the jumper cables? I now had an almost new battery. Yet they might be handy to save some damsel-in-dead-battery-distress next winter. And trust me, there was a whole bunch of other manly truck stuff or, as Marcie called it, "crap and junk" that needed judgment passed on.

Maybe technology and the Internet could help with these important decisions. I laid all the stuff, junk, and crap out on a tarp in the garage and snapped a picture of the pile. I then uploaded the picture to "Facebook" and asked my eighty-four "Friends" for advice.

As expected, not many of the comments were helpful. Most of my so-called "Friends" used this as an excuse to point out what they saw as my flaws and quirks and make fun of my old truck. However, there was one from a favorite nephew that I did take to heart: "Uncle Mike, the pink umbrella. Keep it for sure."

An Early Goose

I'm not much of a fan of the early hunting opportunities sometimes offered to control wildlife populations. I'm not necessarily against them. It just doesn't seem right to be sitting in a duck blind with a shotgun while fighting off mosquitoes and staring at a forest still green without a hint of gold. Call me a hopeless romantic if you will. I'd rather have snowflakes whipping past my head in early November as a flock of bluebills fights an icy wind and foaming whitecaps towards a set of decoys.

Sometimes there is cause for an exception. Today is only September 1. Yet the early goose season meant to thin out the prolific local flock starts at a half-hour before sunrise. Kaliber is now well past twelve years old, well past the average life expectancy of a Labrador Retriever, and well past the usual age of those still able to hunt. The chance to share some quality time is too good to pass up.

Besides that, I sense an opportunity. For the past two mornings, while I was trolling the lake drinking coffee and eating snacks under the guise of fishing, a flock of Canadian geese had lifted off the lake to the east and cruised over Stony Point at treetop level. Honking in chorus, showing no signs of caution—perhaps they need to be wised up and maybe even provide the makings of a family feast.

Kal and I motor to Stony Point under a dark sky with a hint of dawn to the east. A half-dozen floating goose decoys are placed around the point to resemble a contented family gathering. They may not be needed but could offer some encouragement should a non-local goose wander by. Kal is her usual self—excitement and adrenaline overriding the aches and pains of arthritis. She perches on the middle boat seat, tail wagging, whining, and ready for action.

Since the geese will be coming in low from the east, I park the boat on the west side of the point and don't bother with camouflage. That's a benefit of the early season, I guess. These geese should be well used to my red Lund and the dozens of others that ply the same waters with them all summer.

The sun is starting to light up the lake as we settle in beneath the solitary red pine anchoring the narrow rocky point with its roots. There's a hint of fog rising from the lake, a clear indication that the lake is still warmer than the fortyish air temperature. The beaver that lives down the shore makes an appearance, gliding through the lily pads, cutting a rippling V through the still water. I hold Kal by the collar, restraining her as she whines and begs to retrieve. The beaver's unimpressed, stopping ten yards out, eyeing us with his back just breaking the surface, broad tail floating behind. We don't even rate an obligatory tail slap this morning. He just cruises back into the bay with no comment.

The usual sunrise comes and goes with only a couple of wood ducks landing in the decoys in the half light, flying away shrieking when we are spotted. But I've had worse mornings. There's a full Thermos of hot coffee, snacks, the mosquitoes aren't bad, and the sunrise brings a welcome warmth. Kal's restless— shifting weight from one leg to another with the discomfort of her arthritis, unwilling to take the

chance of lying down and missing something exciting.
The geese are supposed to show at around 8 a.m.
That comes and goes with nary a honk. By 8:30 it's
time to try something else. I'm once again convinced
that this early season hunting is not my thing. Just
then there is a honk, a quick chorus from behind to
the north. I spin around and find twenty geese winging
in from the north, using another flight path today.
The exciting burst of honking tells the story. They
have spotted my unprotected back side and that red
boat from three hundred feet in the sky and won't
bother to swing over and check out the decoys. Early
season or not, they aren't taking any chances.

The flock locks wings and glides down toward a
small bay on the far side of the lake, pirouetting in
formation, and touching down with one more burst of
honks. They paddle deeper into the bay and out of
sight while I plot their demise. I can pick up my
decoys, motor over with the boat, and sneak across the
island for an ambush.

I am hurrying to load the boat when another honk
comes from the lake to the east. I scramble in
reverse, trying to get back out of the boat, uncase
the gun, and stuff a shell in each barrel as a wave of
geese clears the far lake shore and bears down on the
point—just like I planned. They split into two flocks
of ten or fifteen, one rounding the point over the
decoys, the other coming at treetop height in loose
formation. I pull the shotgun up on the huge lead bird
and send a big mass of steel shot way too far out in
front of its bill. The gun comes down from the recoil,
the bead settles squarely on the head of the flaring
goose, and a pull of the trigger empties the second
barrel. The goose folds and crashes down into the

cattails at lake's edge.

A second wave of geese is right behind the first, now stroking wings hard, trying to gain altitude and speed. I reload just in time, pick out another goose, and send both barrels off into the blue, leaving the goose unscathed and the faith in my ability with a shotgun once again shaken. I'm left cursing in knee-deep water as the geese hurry on down the lake, honking alarms, and once again educated. Such as it is with hunting. Two hours of inactivity and contemplation, lost in my own thoughts and the beauty of the morning. Thirty seconds of bedlam and wet feet.

Kal crashes into the lake, searching the lily pads around the boat, eager to retrieve. I make sure no more geese are coming and call her over. She didn't see the goose fall but has faith in my commands and busts off through the cattails, arthritis forgotten. Kal sometimes refuses to retrieve geese—bad taste, too big for her smallish frame—I don't know the reason and she isn't talking. This time she struggles backward though the forest of cattails, dragging one monster goose by a wing tip while I urge her on. She makes it to within a couple of feet of the boat, releases her prize, and stands belly-deep in lake water, tail wagging, and proud.

It's likely the biggest goose I've ever shot and will take some special care back in the kitchen. That worry can wait until a family gathering in the cold of the winter. Early, warm, whatever. While this early season stuff may not be as romantic as wind-whipped snowflakes in the face, I've made more memories on Crooked Lake with an old friend.

How to Pick a Puppy

How to Pick a Puppy

Andy, Kaliber, and I were sitting on the deck in our respective comfy chairs, unwinding from a strenuous morning of chasing crappies on Crooked Lake. Spring had sprung. The hummingbirds were back, the trees were leafed out half-way to summer foliage, spring flowers were blooming in the woods, and the frogs in the swamp along the driveway were belting out their love songs. It was a good place to be. Marcie's little red car crunched down the gravel driveway, returning from a grocery-foraging trip to town with my mother. There she got groceries and an idea.

"I saw an ad for puppies on the store's bulletin board," she informed us. "Really cute little things— half miniature poodle, half rat terrier. I don't really want a puppy right now, but I think I'm going to call and check them out. Their picture was really cute."

"So," I said, "you really don't want a puppy. But you are going to call and talk to someone you don't know about a puppy you don't want?"

"Yeah," she said. "It sounds like an interesting mix. They would be small, maybe not shed, and I bet they would be smart. I'm just curious."

I helped her in with the groceries and then refilled my comfy chair next to Andy.

"I bet she goes and gets one. I bet," Andy said. "What does she want with a little dog?"

"Something to keep her company while Kal and I are up here or gone hunting. But she says she doesn't want another dog for a few years."

A few minutes later, Marcie stepped out of the cabin. "I called the guy and talked to him. They don't live that far away. I'm going to go have a look at them. Want to come along?"

"No!" I answered. "You know me. I would bring every one of them home. If you get a puppy, it has to be your decision."

"I'm not going to get one," she said, walking to the car. "I just want to look." She started to get into her car, stopped, and walked back. "I'm going to take a box and a towel with just in case."

So that's how Murri came into our lives. An unscientific pick from a grocery store bulletin board. A fluffy little apricot-tinged mutt that swam in the lake like a Labrador, barked at the neighbors, and kept our feet warm at night for seven years. We have no regrets about those fun years. But perhaps the short span of her life would hint that this was not the best way to choose a puppy. So the next fluffy mutt puppy, Kaffi Mokka, was picked via Internet research—a more modern version of the grocery store bulletin board.

So how do you pick a puppy?

I've had some experience, although I don't remember much about the first. I got a straw-colored Lab puppy for my fourth birthday. I remember going to pick him up but not much about the selection process. Butch was my constant companion on the farm for the next seven years. With a BB gun in my hands, we roamed the woodlot, the pasture, and the farm buildings, intent on extermination of the short list of grain-eating, hay-fouling vermin we were allowed to hunt.

Pigeons, sparrows, and blackbirds were fair game. Song birds were not. Butch and I had to part ways when we moved to town. An independent free-ranging male, he would not have adapted well to city life. It was not an easy break.

There were a couple early and short flings with beagles since then. Great happy, noisy dogs but ones with typical hound dog independence and a low tolerance for swimming and cold-weather hunting. Since then it's been Labrador Retrievers, all black females picked by various methods. The first was Maggie. My landlord did not allow pets. Marcie's did. We weren't married yet but somehow I convinced her, and the girls she lived with, that they needed to start raising a puppy for me. Maggie greeted us with an old bone in her mouth, tail wagging, begging to play with us new strangers. She was the only female in a small litter. The choice was obvious.

We picked Brooke two short days after Maggie's untimely death. The criteria for her selection was simple. She was available, we couldn't imagine life without a dog, and she was playing in a water dish when we met the litter. There wasn't much more thought than that. Brooke turned out to be a pheasant dog with few equals. If there was an old rooster in the cattails, she was going to make him fly. You just had to be close, ready, and accurate.

Brooke was with us for almost eleven years. When her time came, I was determined to seek out the best possible replacement. After looking over several litters, the search led us to a veteran breeder who advised us on choosing a puppy that would be both a good family dog for our two young sons and a good hunter. With her help, we didn't choose one of the hyperactive alpha pups or the fat one that didn't bother to stand up and greet us. Ripley went home with us and fulfilled those family and hunting obligations for another eleven years.

Once Ripley started showing her age, we agreed to get a puppy and have two dogs. That way Rip could help hang out with the puppy and show her the way of the Labrador. With time for research, I looked into the background of several litters before selecting a veteran professional breeder whose dogs I had seen in action. As Marcie and the kids played with a group of prospects, I talked puppy picking with him.

"How do you do it?" I asked. "What makes you pick one over the other?"

"I've seen people try everything," he said. "Families come here and spend hours agonizing over which puppy to take home. Guys come with dead birds or feathers and try to see which puppy acts more interested. I'm convinced none of that makes much difference. I do my research, talk to other breeders— that kind of stuff. But when it comes to actually picking one from a litter, I just walk over, reach down, and pick one up."

We didn't take this simple advice. Kaliber was picked because she had the shiniest coat of the two females that followed us around the kennel yard.

Almost fourteen years later, I started shopping for the next dog while still grieving from the loss of my longtime companion. This research didn't help much. Mainly because prices for well-bred Labradors seemed to have skyrocketed while I enjoyed Kal's company and the females were often gone before I worked up the will to call. Then a litter popped up on the Internet in a town not far away. "Family-raised," the ad said.

"Great hunters," it said. I made the call, actually sent a text, determined not to look at them and get suckered in by puppy eyes before I was sure they met my standards. We exchanged texts and emails. The bloodlines looked good. The owner sounded knowledgeable. The price was right. So we made the trip to look the litter over.

A fifteen-year-old girl greeted Marcie and me at her family's hobby farm and showed us a dozen black puppies she was selling to pad her college fund. She might as well have been selling Girl Scout cookies. We took the five available females out on a porch and sat down with them. One crawled into my lap and started chewing my sweatshirt. Two more went to work on my shoelaces. At that point my eyes started to mist up. Perhaps part from missing my old friend Kal. Perhaps part from the anticipation of once again having a puppy in my life. I grabbed the sweatshirt chewer and stood up.

"We'll take this one," I said. "Her name is Sage."

S.O.L.

I always hesitate to publish a fishing or hunting story that takes place on Crooked Lake. Some readers might infer that I am some sort of expert and show up with an army of buddies to share my hidden hotspot. Expert or not, and I swear this is not a fib, Crooked Lake is only an average lake when it comes to either sport. Think you are going to net the next world record walleye here? Not likely. If you brag about catching even one walleye in front of my dock, I'll ask to see the evidence in high resolution video. Think you're going to get your limit of mallards here while watching a spread of decoys on some October morning? Not likely. Not on Crooked Lake. You would be outa luck on both those wishes.

So why am I cruising across Crooked Lake in the dark of a cold October morning, loaded with shotgun, duck decoys, and an inexperienced Labrador puppy? Because it's here. The lake. The possibility of a duck or two. The hope of a nice sunrise with an eagle floating past. And besides, I got a new puppy to break in. Sage is riding on the middle seat of the Lund, all decked out in her borrowed puppy-sized camo coat, one she might outgrow before the end of the season. Any excursion with a new pup is bound to be an adventure and may be worth a few laughs even on a poor lake.

The boat rounds the corner of Bird Island, red/green bow light pointed toward Stony Point. It looks like the day is off to a good start. No other boat lights are in sight and nobody waves a flashlight from the Point to warn us off. Now the fun begins. Tossing duck decoys from a boat with a Lab puppy can be an exercise that involves yelling "NO! NO!" and then getting soaked with October-temperature lake water as an anxious and dripping wet, decoy-retrieving puppy is hauled back into the boat. In this case, Sage's puppy obedience class training proves its worth. I tell her "OFF!" and drop a decoy in. Then repeat the process. She remains in her seat, interested, watching the decoys splash into the dark water by the light of my headlamp. So far, so good. Not willing to push my luck, I quit at a meager twelve decoys and push the boat onto shore still dry and warm.

Now comes one of the best parts of duck hunting. Sitting down on a seat cushion, snuggling deep into a warm parka, and pouring the first cup of coffee. The ducks, if they come, won't be legal targets for another fifteen minutes. We've got time to relax and enjoy the sunrise. Sage roams the narrow point, exploring its rocky confines, and checking out all the great smells left behind by the local wildlife and previous hunters. She roots around in the grass and makes her first retrieve of the day, proudly presenting me with an empty red plastic shotgun shell, one that I, or some other guy, carelessly left behind days ago.

What Crooked Lake lacks for waterfowl, it makes up for with other wildlife and some of it isn't shy. The beaver is the first to show. Cruising just outside the farthest decoy, eying us with suspicion. The bunch that lives in the lodge down the shore is busy reworking the landscape. The islands and lake shore used to be hosts to leafy aspens, birch, and willows.

Not anymore. Not since the resurgence of beaver populations years ago. Any remaining non-evergreen trees seem destined to be breakfast, lunch, and dinner for the local beavers. Even mighty oaks are being ringed by buck teeth in the dark of the night. Bird Island is now covered with bushy spruce and tall pyramid-shaped Norway pine that don't seem to be a food source. One wonders what food source or lake is slated for ruin next. This critter swims back down in the bay, no doubt with further evil tree-cutting in mind.

A less-destructive seasonal resident swims over for a look as dawn starts to break. This juvenile loon appears to be the last of his kind on the lake for this year. There's always at least one. Loons seem to be the best of parents during the summer. They hatch two or three chicks from the nest back in the floating bog, keep the youngsters close at hand, and feed them and protect them from the resident eagles that seem to prefer young loon over all other tasty bits.

It's a good year when several broods hatch and at least a couple chicks make it to September. By then the adult loons seem to have lost all parental instincts. They head south to the Caribbean for a winter of rest and relaxation, leaving the young behind to eat, fly, and migrate on their own. The youngsters won't leave until ice is coating the shores and there are no options. This one seems lonely, swimming in and out of our duck decoys, uttering muted hoots that aren't returned by our plastic fakes.

Sage watches the loon, eager to try a retrieve if given the word. That's already better than the last dog. Kal loved duck hunting and retrieving even in the coldest weather. Her methods were different. She would pace the point, whining, watching the sky and the decoys for the slightest suspicious move, unwilling to sit back and observe like Sage. And she routinely chased beavers and loons while I shouted bad things at her.

Our first action comes as the sun breaks the horizon and lights up the decoys with a warm golden glow. Two ring-neck ducks zip in unseen from the north and skid to a landing outside the farthest decoy. They try to leave just as fast, jumping into the southern breeze and heading out low across the water. I manage to get the small 20-gauge double-barrel up in time and drop the first one to the water with the right barrel. Steel shot from the second barrel ripples the water well behind the second duck as it escapes.

Sage doesn't hesitate. Puppy or not, she does what comes naturally for her breed and crashes into the water, whining with excitement as she paddles out to the duck, grabs it, and circles around back to the point. She's not perfect yet. I have to chase her around the point and retrieve the warm body from her. It's a nice dark blue and snow-white drake, a good start to the day.

The bright, early sun and the light breeze are indicators that the duck flight will be short this morning. With no cold weather, ice, or snow in the forecast, all the local ducks can pick any pond in the forest to hang out on. But a few are willing to give our decoys a look. A half a dozen little bufflehead buzz past, circle, and then leave without coming in range. A pair of the same comes from behind and flies away unscathed despite two quick blasts from the shotgun. Then one of those moments we duck hunters live for happens.

A lone drake mallard comes over high and out of range. I quack the lonely quack of a hen mallard several times. He circles high, looking for company. I quack again. He responds with a slow circling turn over the main lake with Sage alert and watching beside me. Wings cup into the wind and he descends from on high, decision made, no turning back, the white band separating his green head and chestnut breast standing out in the morning sun. For once I don't mess the opportunity up. The shotgun booms, he crumples, and splashes down into the decoys.

Sage launches herself from the bank, making a much mightier splash than the duck. I watch with pride; this little dog is learning fast. She completes her retrieve by grabbing the decoy nearest the still body of the duck and struggling back to shore, decoy in mouth, dragging the anchor and whining the whole way. That's okay. She's still just a pup. I resort to a time-honored technique for us non-professional retriever trainers. A walnut-sized rock from the shoreline is pitched out near the duck, making an attention-grabbing splash. Sage leaps back in and gets it right this time, delivering the big, beautiful duck right to my hand.

There's no more ducks in the air after that. Which is just as well. We've had a good morning, a better than average day on an average lake and it's time for some bonding. If any ducks do come winging by, it's their lucky day. Cause I'm sort of S.O.L.— have a bad case of Sage-On-Lap.

Mysteries of the Northwoods

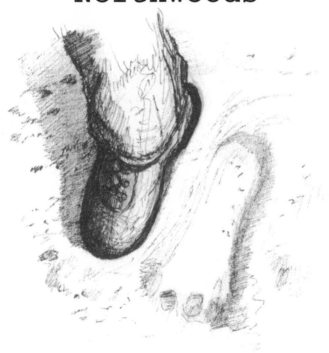

Life in the North Country, deep in the woods, is full of mysteries. Some big, some small, some solvable, some likely not. Some important. Others not so important. What was that small brownish bird that flitted across the driveway, into the bushes, not to be seen again? What sort of animal left that pile of "stuff" on the end of the dock? Was that odd huge ripple on the otherwise calm surface of the lake just a stray wind gust? Or was it the Crooked Lake version of the Loch Ness monster? Some are even more mysterious, when under the cloak of darkness, they howl, screech, rustle, or go bump in the night.

Most of these can be answered by patience, research or both. Take the strange jungle-monkey-type calls straight out of a Tarzan movie that echo across the channel from Big Island around sundown or a little before. Just about the same time as the barred owls are calling "Who cooks for you, who cooks for you, who cooks for youooooooooooo." I dug around in nature books and websites and found these calls attributed to young barred owls experimenting with their untried voices.

Most of these encounters are harmless and only evoke a sense of mystery or a need for more knowledge. Not a sense of fear. But not all. On a late March morning, Sage and I took advantage of the above freezing temperatures and the melting snow to venture into the forest on the first hike of spring. Sage led the way, happy to be free from the confines of the

171

cabin, doing her Labrador thing, quartering back and forth down the trail perhaps twenty yards in front. All was well until we approached a south-facing hillside cloaked in a dense stand of pines.

Sage stopped in the middle of the trail, head up, tail straight out, staring ahead into the pines. I stopped and waited, wondering what she was sensing, searching the dark hillside with my much inferior senses. She lifted her nose, tested the wind, and then did something my other dogs have never done. She trotted back to my side, pressed up against a leg, and continued staring back at the hillside. Now Sage can't talk any better than most other Labrador Retrievers, but the message was as clear as spoken words—"Mike, there's something up there I don't want to mess with!" And if she didn't want to mess with it, neither did I. Armed only with a hiking stick, I considered my options, decided against further investigation and retreated.

Sage was only a year old when this happened— still somewhat of a pup. But in that year she had roamed these woods with me many times, had encounters with deer, smelled fresh bear poop, coyote poop, wolf poop—all sorts of wild stinky stuff—and never reacted with any sign of fear or concern. A good guess would be that it was an early rising bear or wolf or wolves, so near and not so warm and fuzzy that she reacted with more concern than to just a pile of warm poo. Then again, who's to say it wasn't one of those creepy things from the old horror movies I used to watch before I started spending so much time alone in the woods? Perhaps an even stranger theory might be one I have been reluctant to write much about, given the possibility of being labeled just another Northwoods kook or a wanna-be Reality TV show host.

Several years ago, the sunlight was shining bright on a March morning, a vague hint of the spring yet to come as Crooked Lake was still entombed in a foot and a half of ice. I ventured out, hiking the slippery surface, wandering in and out of the islands, prospecting for other signs of spring. Many of the North Country's critters were doing the same. The beavers were splashing and chirping in their mansion-sized hut on the northern shore of Bird Island. Sandhill cranes were trilling their prehistoric dinosaur-like calls off to the south. Geese and swans honked and trumpeted overhead. All kinds of other creatures were using the lake as a highway while they still could.

At a narrow channel between the mainland and island, a flurry of tracks marred the trace of snow clinging near shore. A pair of mink had crossed the channel together—mating time for these usually solitary creatures? A lone fisher had hugged the shore, weaving in and out of the rocks and logs, perhaps searching the melting shore for crayfish, frogs, or winter-killed fish. A red squirrel had hip-hopped out to investigate an ice-bound pinecone and then scurried back. Spring was on the way and all these and more were anxious to get on with life.

Halfway across the channel, in a small patch of drifted crusty snow, I came upon the new mystery. There, vaguely outlined in the sugary snow, was a long and narrow imprint. It was wider at the front and narrower at the back, although determining front and back required an obvious leap of faith. The wider "front" to the track had a series of indentations— almost like toe prints, you might say. It stretched slightly larger than my size eleven insulated hiking boot.

Yes, I think you're getting the picture. This mark in the snow resembled a large, say size thirteen or fourteen, barefoot human footprint. A big barefoot human footprint, in late March, in the crunchy snow of a frozen lake, a long way from any cabin.

There was only one track, captured in that random patch of wind-driven snow surrounded by hard, slick-surfaced ice. There may be some rational, logical explanations. Like an early rising bear with a large, skinny deformed foot. Or my neighbor Marv playing a joke, hoping to generate a call to the authorities and an interesting note in the local newspaper's police report. Or more likely Mother Nature playing tricks with sunshine and melting snow to create a playful ruse just to keep us humans wondering.

I'll keep you posted while trying to sort out this Northwoods mystery. Hopefully there is a logical, rational, and happy explanation. Then again, my spouse Marcie, a well-educated and usually logical, rational person, was willing to articulate a not-so-rational logical possibility when shown the picture of my boot planted alongside the mystery track. "Well," she said, "it looks like Big Foot forgot to wear his flip-flops last night."

Firewood
Happens—Again

I know I have used this line before, but bear with me please. Any Northwoods cabin should have a wood-burning fireplace or stove, whether it's just to take the bite out of the indoor air on chilly mornings or as a main source of heat for the winter. If your significant other, budget or insurance person won't allow one, I hope for heaven's sake you at least have a campfire ring to sit around and discuss big topics with the neighbors. In any case, you are going to need some firewood.

My methods of obtaining firewood have varied over the years. I've harvested trees from my own property. I've hunted down and purchased slab wood from local sawmills. I've foraged for logging leftovers in the state forest—with the proper permits, of course. I might even have stolen a downed tree once —my memory is a little hazy on that affair. All these methods work subject to their pros and cons and levels of effort.

For a while, buying slab wood from sawmills seemed like the preferred method when the home-grown supply ran low. It didn't involve the danger of trees falling the wrong way and crushing personnel or personal property. The price was right. I met new, hard-working people with unique personalities and still got some quality time with the chainsaw while cutting the slabs to stove length. Then I started to miss the thrill of the hunt, the drama, the suspense and the intense competition involved in foraging for wood in the state forest.

Most of the wood available in the state forest comes in the form of leftovers from logging operations. Loggers cut down and harvest the trees they are told to or have paid for and then sort out the ones with commercial value. Not every oak or aspen or every part of every oak or aspen may have commercial value. The loggers leave behind the non-valuable leftovers. The local Forestry Office then issues a limited number of permits for "fuel wood" for each logging site. As long as you have the permit, some of that leftover wood is yours for the taking.

Sounds simple enough, except that I'm not the only cabin or home owner in the area that needs firewood. Competition for the good stuff can be fierce. The level of competition depends on many factors including the price of other heating fuels. In a year when natural gas or propane prices are high, lots of Northwoods dwellers think wood—especially cheap wood from the forest. Then come the other factors—the type of wood, how easy it is to access and, to a certain degree, the time of the year.

Most seasoned wood-burners know that hardwoods like oak, maple, and ash are the gold standards of Northwoods firewood. These are "the good stuff." The ones that provide high heat content per stick and are the first to get hauled away. As far as accessibility, not all logging sites are created equal. Some may be miles away down minimum maintenance forest roads and then more miles down rutted temporary logging roads. When it comes to the time of the year, most people, sometimes myself included, don't tend to think too hard about firewood supplies until the first frost on the truck's windshield sends a reminder. Thus an easy-to-access logging site, close to the cabin, with lots of oak, maple, and ash is a hot commodity come September or October. My request for a permit from the friendly folks at the Forestry Office might be turned down. Some of those pesky neighbors beat me to the punch.

I do have several advantages over most other firewood foragers. One, I don't have a respectable day job anymore. So at least in theory, my firewood season runs seven days a week, 365 days a year. I also have an advantage with local intelligence. My neighbor Marv is a full-time resident who, like me, has no respectable day job. He likes to rumble down forest roads in his old jeep with his morning coffee. All I need to do is mention that firewood is running low. He now has a purpose to the jeep rides and starts patrolling the woods, evaluating multiple logging sites for firewood potential. He then takes me on a drive to view the short list. With this info in hand, I race to the Forestry Office and apply for a permit before the lazy and less informed.

Marv's also good about reminding me that others might be after the same air-dried pile of oak that he spotted. While others might take the summer off from firewood accumulation, I feel compelled to use Marv's info and get the stuff hauled back to the cabin site before a cold snap sends my competitors into the woods with trucks, trailers, and chainsaws. There's a certain lawless element out there that factors in too. Not everyone in the North Country plays by the same set of rules. A nice pile of easily accessible oak has been known to disappear from a site before the local authorities have issued a single permit. That adds further uncertainty and competition to the process.

While the lack of a day job adds to the hours and days of firewood season, I do have a handicap worth mentioning. I'm not as young as I used to be and thus take longer to accumulate firewood than my competitors who maybe don't qualify for the Senior Discount at the local grocery store on Thursdays. I might be out there chainsawing in June, fighting the mosquitoes, deer flies, wood ticks, and black flies while my competition is working or trolling the local lakes for walleyes. But my loads are smaller and farther apart.

Marv recently tipped me off to a nearby logging site with plenty of oak stacked down a not-too-badly rutted logging road. I raced to the local DNR office, got the first permit issued for the site, and proceeded to use a week in late June to haul six-foot lengths of prime oak back to the cabin. I soon had enough quality wood for a year. I didn't stop there, hauling more, piling the stuff near the outhouse until I had a two-year supply. Then I got greedy. I went back again and again, stacking my trailer with oak until my back cried for mercy.

I took a break, cold beer in hand, to admire my wealth, gloat about beating the competition, and to plan the massive amount of work yet ahead. The oversized stack of logs still needed to be chainsawed to length, split by hand, stacked, and covered to start the drying process. With some luck, no mechanical problems, and no major physical ailments, I might be done by the time the lake froze. That's the problem with firewood; it really doesn't grow on trees.

A Practical Guide to Lawn Mowing for Cabin Owners

I haven't done a scientific poll on this subject, but given over twenty years of practical experience and some hearsay, I think I know the number one reason why some cabin owners sell out after a short residence time and move on to a motorhome, a condo, or forget about recreational living altogether. It's not what you might think: not the property taxes, not the long weekend commute, or even the unruly neighbors. It's mowing the cabin lawn.

The typical cabin owner shows up on Friday evening, just before dark, and there it is: a lawn that's a foot tall and full of mosquitoes and wood ticks. Replanting the flowers the deer ate and replacing the bird feeders the bears twisted and savaged can wait for a trip to the garden center in the morning. But relaxing on the deck with a cup of coffee first thing in the morning isn't the same if you are staring at a jungle of grass and fighting the hordes of bugs living in it. It's got to be dealt with pronto before the descending darkness obscures all the stumps, tree roots, rocks and other obstacles typical of a cabin yard.

The choice of lawnmower is critical to success. Thinking about a big, new, expensive self-propelled lawnmower capable of hacking down the lawn at warp speed? Sounds good at first. But pretty soon you're wondering why there's a better lawnmower at the cabin than at home. And big, new, expensive lawnmowers also have lots of parts to break and fail. Like electric starters and batteries. A solar charger clipped to the battery while you are gone for weeks at a time will help. Just be aware that it won't stop the red squirrels and chipmunks from chewing the wires off and rendering it start-less. Most expensive mowers also have some sort of drive mechanism or transmission that is guaranteed to freeze up or break under the strain of cabin lawn mowing.

On the other hand, a garage sale lawnmower has many things going for it. Cheap price, cheap disposal when you hit a stump or forget to check the oil, and readily replaceable at the next garage sale across the lake. Once again, my experience tells me they do have disadvantages. If repairs are needed, you will discover that reasonably priced small engine repairmen are hard to find these days and parts for a thirty-year-old garage sale mower might not be available. The time wasted trying to start, fix, or replace can cut into recreational time—which is really what having a lake place or woodsy cabin is all about, isn't it?

So, twenty years into this experiment, I have settled on a middle-of-the-road option—a new no-frills lawnmower from the local farm store. These cost about $150 and can be counted on to last a couple years, thus roughly equaling the price of several years' worth of garage sale lawnmowers. They also come with a few added bonuses. The new mower is likely to have a sharp blade for the first few trips around the yard and safety features not found on the typical old lawnmower. If you are willing to be vague as to the cause of the first few repairs, the farm store might even honor the warranty.

A word about blades here—don't bother to ever sharpen them. Never. Never ever. It's a losing battle.

The previously mentioned hazards of rocks, stumps, and tree roots will dull them faster that they can be sharpened. And taking a blade off to sharpen it will expose you to a major hazard that you won't think of until it's too late. Somewhere in the cabin lawn lurks at least one poison ivy plant. The lawnmower blade becomes contaminated with the poisonous juice every time the lawn is mowed. Removing the blade for sharpening is a sure way to rub the oils deep into your skin and create the worst case of poison ivy ever imagined. Just let the dull blade hack away and recycle it with the rest of the mower when that sad final moment comes.

So let's review these tips before one final word. Some lawn mowing is a necessary evil, even if you leave most of your property natural like me. Get used to it or stay home. Take your time, mount a handy cup holder so you can enjoy yourself, pick an old lawnmower or a new cheap one, and don't fret about the cost of repairs. Bad things are going to happen to the mower. Don't go getting personally attached to your latest victim.

Now for my final advice. The lawn is going to look a little ragged after you mow it the first time. After all, it was a foot tall, you used a cheap lawnmower with a dull blade, and you maybe even mowed it after dark while using a headlamp for guidance. So go over it one more time on Sunday afternoon just before you leave. That way the bears, the deer, the chipmunks, and the squirrels will have beautifully manicured grass to enjoy while you head home to mow the lawn there.

Cabin Talk

Random seating at a fundraiser placed me alongside a ten-year-old boy and his father. The occasion was the annual spring luncheon held by the Listening Point Foundation in honor of the late writer and naturalist Sigurd F. Olson. The foundation exists to preserve Sigurd's legacy of wilderness education, his home and writing shack in Ely, and the land and cabin he called Listening Point on Burntside Lake. Other attendees around us were discussing personal experiences with Listening Point and opening up family cabins for another summer of fun. I asked the youngster if he had a cabin.

He started slow. "We have a place on a lake up by Ely." I pressed him for the name of the lake, and when he offered it up, told him of my adventures near there. He warmed up and went on to describe his favorite activities, typical boy stuff—swimming, fishing off the dock, and catching crayfish along the shore. This was enlightening information coming from a boy his age, in this era of smartphones, video games, and social media. "Maybe there is hope for the younger generation," I thought, echoing the thoughts of many an old codger before me. I asked him for more details on his cabin. His father listened in, smiling at the conversation and the interaction.

"I wouldn't really call it a cabin," the kid offered reluctantly, seemingly a bit embarrassed by the situation. "It's pretty big."

This young man, as innocent and inexperienced as

he was, had somehow picked up on the nuances of the term "cabin," a word that has suffered a bit definition-wise lately. For example, when I mention my lake cabin, many people jump to the conclusion that it's a spacious log lodge with all the amenities. Maybe they assume that since my spouse Marcie and I qualify as "Seniors," we've moved beyond the hassles of the simple life. In reality, our cabin measures only 16 feet x 20 feet—much smaller than most modern day suburban garages. Neighbors have been known to refer to it as "The Wee House." While it does have electricity, the necessities of life are taken care of by a small woodstove and an outhouse.

All the dictionaries I have checked are similar in defining the term "cabin." A 1970 vintage American Heritage Dictionary on a shelf above my writing desk defines a cabin as "a small roughly built house." A newer 1996 version agrees with that. The up-to-date Merriam-Webster electronic dictionary built into my computer takes it one step further—"a small one-story dwelling usually of simple construction." Further digging provides the interesting factoid (if you can believe the Internet) that the word "cabin" is derived from the 14th Century Medieval Latin term "capanna" or hut.

These definitions are pretty straightforward and seem to match the description of my simple structure. Except that mine is actually two stories and, having labored mightily while constructing it, I take exception to the "roughly built" part of the first definition. I may not be a master craftsman but some of the friends and family that helped during critical parts of the construction are and I am pretty darn happy with the end result.

I wonder if Henry David Thoreau, one of the oldest and most famous of American cabin writers, might also have taken umbrage to this "roughly built" term. He built the cabin that was immortalized in his classic *Walden* from trees cut with a borrowed axe, some recycled lumber, and minimal amounts of purchased items like nails and hinges. The 10x15-foot structure included a rock hearth and chimney he built from local materials. The total cash outlay came to 28 dollars and 12 1/2 cents in 1846.

While the cabin was obviously important as his main abode and the fruit of some hard labor, the book itself does not linger long on architecture or interior design details. The main focus is the surrounding environment: the plants, trees, critters, the pond, and the simple life style he espouses to at length. The book is a difficult read for modern folks, with antiquated and laborious language by today's standards. However, stick with it and gems of wisdom are discovered as he advertises the simple life. One of my favorites does involve the cabin and the construction cost: "I thus found that the student who wishes for a shelter can obtain one for a lifetime at an expense not greater than the rent which he now pays annually." Here's another quote that sums up life at my cabin and hopefully others: "Why should we live with such hurry and waste of life?"

This lack of dwelling on the structure itself carries through to other famous and more modern cabin writers: Aldo Leopold, for example. He purchased an old Wisconsin farm in 1935 and wrote extensively about the land and his activities in *A Sand County Almanac*. Published in 1949 just after his death and almost a hundred years after Thoreau's *Walden*, the book is still required reading for most formal naturalist and wildlife management courses. You have to search long and hard and in other places to find information about his cabin. In fact, while he calls it a cabin in his book, he most often refers to it as "The Shack" in his other writings. Research outside the book says it was actually an old chicken coop remodeled to serve as a cabin. One picture shows a garage-sized structure, clad in weathered board siding with a lean-to added on. It looks like it fits that formal definition of a small one-story shelter.

The third chapter, titled "Great Possessions," is a great read for any cabin owner. Sitting on his front porch at 3:30 a.m. on a July morning, with a pot of coffee and notebook, he chronicles the bird calls as they awake to the early light. First, a field sparrow at 3:35. Then a robin shortly after, followed by an oriole. Once the world is fully awake and the coffee pot empty, he and his dog set off on a rambling walk to survey their domain. This is an experience I've often replicated from my cabin deck as the world wakes up before sunrise in the northern Minnesota forest.

Back to Sigurd Olson and the Listening Point cabin. I've been there many times, both in group settings when history flows from knowledgeable tour guides and by myself for quiet contemplation. The cabin is a simple structure that for much of its original life was actually a chicken coop—almost eerily like Leopold's "Shack." Sig discovered the abandoned structure on a local farm "with the roof still sound and the logs silvery-gray." It was carefully dismantled and most of the logs moved to that special spot on Burntside Lake for reassembly and the addition of windows and fireplace. The recycled and weathered chicken-coop-turned-cabin was just what he was looking for: "We wanted red squirrels spiraling down the trunks of the pine and vaulting onto the roof as though it were part of the trees themselves."

Those two quotes are from Sigurd's second book, *Listening Point*, which describes the process of finding the ideal undeveloped land, bringing in the access road, and choosing the actual cabin site. But once again, like Thoreau and Leopold, the cabin plays second fiddle to the natural setting, adventures in the surrounding territory, and the simple life. The cabin itself is only mentioned in passing in most chapters.

Sounds simple enough. However, to call the Listening Point cabin "roughly built" would be an insult to the original Finnish carpenters who painstakingly fitted the logs and notched dovetailed corners of the cabin together with Old World craftsmanship. The current craftsmen that maintain its timeless simple beauty would likely also not be pleased.

So that brings us back around to that argument or question. What really is a cabin? How big can it be? How many stories? How "fancy built"? If we heed the words of these famous authors, maybe we shouldn't be worrying about size or construction or appearance. Maybe it is a one-story hand-built structure like the *Walden* cabin or a remodeled chicken coop like Mr. Leopold's "Shack" or the Listening Point cabin. Or maybe it's a many-roomed log lodge worthy of the cover of a glossy ten-dollar magazine on the front row of the newsstand. What appears to matter most to these icons of American nature and cabin writing is what goes on around the cabin, not the cabin itself.

That said, I have to think that stoic old Henry

David Thoreau, Mr. Simple Living himself, would have approved of the final exchange between the youngster and his dad at the fund raiser. His father made a reasonable closing argument. "It doesn't matter how big it is," he stated. "We can call it a cabin if we want to."

However, that didn't match the logic of the son's response—"Dad, we can't call it a cabin," he objected. "It has air conditioning!"

EXTRAS!

Fiction

I don't write much fiction. But when I do, it usually wins an award . . .

Sorry for the shameless self-promotion there. In my defense, shameless self-promotion is one of the first skills a writer needs to learn.

"A River Runs Through It" won First Place for Fiction in the 2013 Jackpine Writers' Bloc competition for the anthology *The Talking Stick 22*.

A River Runs Through It

The Crow Wing River is a quiet Minnesota river, flowing smoothly over a weedy sand bottom, not thundering, tumbling downhill over boulders like a mountain trout stream. Fifty years ago, Grandpa's cabin was barely visible to river travelers, tucked away in the woods above, only noticeable due to the short wooden dock protruding from the shore. If I remember things right, most of my childhood was spent sprawled out on that dock, the rough-sawn wood prickling the bare skin of my stomach, and the sun burning my back.

The grassy weeds on the sand bottom beneath the dock waved back and forth with the rhythm of the current, periodically offering glimpses of the hiding places of crayfish, minnows, and fish. Hypnotized by the flow of the river, it was easy then to dream about jumping into the canoe and escaping downriver from Nimrod—floating past Motley and Brainerd in the dark, undetected. Past the glaring lights of industrial parks of "The Cities," all the way to the freedom and novelty of the ocean. I didn't really want to escape from the cabin or dock. But it was an adventure worth dreaming about.

Just a rotted post or two of the old dock remains now, half-submerged and hidden by the reeds at water's edge. I was back now, on a new dock, with a new dream.

She hadn't said much. This was her first time in this strange place and, let's be honest, we hadn't spent much time together. She held my hand with her left, clutched her pink Barbie fishing pole with her right, and considered the river, bright brown eyes taking in the green expanse, long dark hair blowing across that perfect face.

Barely four years old, she had already experienced considerable turmoil, more than I ever had as a kid. I wondered if she was confused by life so far, or didn't even think about it. I had noticed that she didn't know what to call me. What do you call a sort of unofficial step-grandfather? I knew one thing for sure: I really wanted her to like me.

"It's a big river, isn't it?" I said breaking the silence.

"No, it's not. It's just a little river," she replied with her usual contrariness.

"But it is," I said. "This river follows all the way down past your grandpa's house, past your house, gets even bigger, and ends up in the ocean where the Little Mermaid and all her friends live. She could swim here if she wanted to. You might catch her with your Barbie pole."

I immediately regretted that last comment. I think I was trying too hard

She looked at me like I was the dumbest old guy on earth. "No, I couldn't—she's too big. And Ariel doesn't eat worms!" She pointed to the white Styrofoam container of "icky" nightcrawlers we had purchased last night in Motley.

I sat down on the smooth, cool, plastic decking of the new dock and tried another movie. "Let's see what does eat them. Maybe you can catch Nemo, that goofy little fish."

"No, I can't. Nemo lives in Australia."

"Well, maybe. But I've seen a turtle over there on that log that looks a lot like Nemo's pal Crunch."

"His name is Crush," she said. "And he doesn't live here either."

My knowledge of kid movies was limited and starting to show. It was time to try another angle. "Okay, Princess, I think you watch too many movies. Lie down on the dock and let's see what does live here."

That brought a smile. She did like the nickname I had chosen for her and never fought that. She flopped down beside me, a bit clumsy in her tight pink lifejacket, and peered down into the gold sand and green weeds of the river. I kept my mouth shut and waited for a reaction.

"I don't see anything," she said after a moment. "Just grass and dirt."

"The fish are here," I insisted. "Right there in the weeds. I know them by name—Red Eye is my favorite. He's a Rocker."

She looked up from the water with a dubious look in those serious brown eyes. "A Rocker?"

"A rock bass. I call them 'Rockers' because they look cool and have red eyes. You know, like Mick Jagger."

That got another dumb look. I quit talking, pried the lid off the bait container, and grabbed the first wiggling reddish-brown crawler that was unlucky enough to be on top of the bedding.

"You have to be ready." I threaded the squirming bait onto the hot-pink hook we had picked out at the bait store. "Red Eye is always hungry. I'll cast it out."

"No!" She sat up, almost rolling off the side of

the dock, reaching for the pole. "I've been practicing —I can do it!"

She swung the short pole back, readying the cast. The pink and white bobber attached to the line would have smacked me in the face, right between the eyes. But having spent hours on this dock with two sons during an earlier phase of my life, I was ready and ducked in time. It sailed out across the water and splashed into the slow current five feet from the dock. The bobber had hardly righted itself when a bright green shadow rose up out of the weeds and inhaled the sinking nightcrawler.

It was an epic battle of man or, in this case, kid versus fish. The green rock bass pulling the pink bobber under the dock and down around through the weeds, clearly visible in the clean water of the river. My little princess squealed as she cranked the reel, encumbered by the puffy foam lifejacket. I held onto the back of that lifejacket to keep her from stepping off the dock. It all came together when she jerked back on the short pole and brought the six-inch fish flying out of the water and flopping onto the dock.

I pressed the flopper to the dock before it did much damage and grabbed it by a toothless lip. I gently wormed the hook out and presented it to her— half a foot of gleaming green and gold scales with dime-sized blood-red eyes.

"See why I call him Red Eye?"

"Why are his eyes all bloody?" she asked as a small finger reached out, bright pink nail polish meeting wet green scales.

"That's just the way they come—how come your dog has black eyes?"

She gave me that dumb old guy look again. "He has black fur—he's supposed to have black eyes."

"Well, okay—let's just let him go quick. Watch out, he might splash you!" She lay down on the dock, watching closely as I slid Red Eye into the water. Free again, the fish darted back down to the weeds and disappeared.

She watched the weeds waving slowly with the river's flow, dipping her fingers in the warm water, feeling the current rippling past them. I waited for her to make the next move.

She rolled over and reached up for the pole. "Paul—let's try again! I need another worm!"

I got busy, reached for a new victim from the bait container, and kept my mouth shut. At least I had a name now. This clearly was time for a little less talk and a lot more action.

Brigadoon

The canoe headed sidewise against the river's current again as we struggled upstream. "Damn it, Shelly! Paddle harder! No—not the right side! Left! Left!"

She looked back over a bare, bronzed shoulder, sweat streaking her face. "Shut up, Brad! You're the one that got us here—lost at NIMROD!"

A deep voice, shouting down from above, took us by surprise—"Hey, Yellow Canoe! Need a drink and a rest?"

We almost rolled the canoe as we swiveled in unison towards the voice. Sitting high up on the bank, in one of a row of high-backed chairs was a handsome gray-haired guy, smiling, obviously amused by our predicament.

I hesitated. Shelly didn't. "Paddle for the bank —I'm done!"

The guy gave us a hand up the steep bank and introduced himself. "I'm Jerry—welcome to Brigadoon. You want a beer or a water?"

We both opted for the beer. He walked off across the lawn while we surveyed the surroundings from the comfort of the chairs. "What's that name mean?" I asked Shelly. "I've heard it before."

"I think it's like a myth or something—a magical place in Ireland. Or maybe Scotland," she answered.

The place did have a mythical look. The vast expanse of lawn was shaded by mature trees that defeated the hot July sun. The filtered light gave the whole place a golden glow. There was a sweet-looking house with a high peaked roof and a glass-covered front facing the river. Farther back was a garage and two small barns complete with four or five horses and a couple cows with wide upturned horns and shaggy hair the color of a Golden Retriever. Adding to the ambiance was a small group of multicolored chickens free-ranging, scratching for bugs. They didn't look like the type that Colonel Sanders serves up.

I would have loved to explore the place, especially that house, but we politely kept our seats. We must have looked thirsty. Jerry came back with two cans of beer for each of us. Tagging along was a little black dog with a fluffy tail that he introduced as Sophia. He handed off the beers while she checked out the great smells we brought with us.

"Where're you headed? Most people canoe downstream around here."

I gulped half my first beer before answering. "I found a real nice camping spot about ten years ago—a nice island with a sandy beach. A bunch of high school buddies and I spent a week canoeing down the river. I remember it being just upstream from Nimrod. So I figured Shelly and I could paddle up to it, spend the weekend relaxing, and then just float back to town."

"I think that's still upriver—but not too far," Jerry said. "The river's a little high and fast but you should be able to reach it before dark."

Shelly sat back in her chair with Sophia in her lap, sipping beer, and enjoying the breeze off the river while Jerry and I made more small talk. I could have sat there all day with a few more beers and really wanted to ask for a tour of the place. But I

figured we had better move on before Shelly decided my
island was a myth and insisted on turning back
downstream to civilization.

Jerry helped us shove off into the current while
Sophia waded in to cool her feet. "Good luck," he
said. "Stop in on the way back—if you can find us!"

We paddled hard for almost another hour before
it finally appeared, splitting the river in a wide
flat spot. Jerry must have fibbed a bit, using
positive reinforcement to keep us moving. We set up
the tent on the sand beach just as the sun finished
sinking below the trees. We followed suit and sank
into our sleeping bags, exhausted from fighting the
river all afternoon.

The next day was the perfect summer day, 75
degrees, sunny, with just enough breeze to keep the
bugs at bay. We alternated between sitting on the
beach and exploring the clear water for clams, frogs,
and bugs just like a couple of kids on their first
field trip. We built a campfire towards dark and
watched nightfall happen on the river—stately herons
flying past in slow motion, ducks zooming downriver to
somewhere, and a damn big snapping turtle that started
to haul out on "our" beach, then retreated as fast as
a turtle can at the crackle of the fire.

We had a little wine. We watched and listened to
the river. We had one magical night as we watched the
sparks from the campfire float up into the clear night
sky until they mingled with the stars.

A thick fog blanketed the river bottom in the
morning. We brewed a pot of coffee over the coals of
last night's fire, then packed up and headed
downstream, drifting with the current. I watched for
the bank and the chairs that would mark Brigadoon. I

thought I heard a rooster crow once in the fog behind us. But between the current hurrying us downstream and the fog muffling sound and robbing sense of direction and place, we must have missed it somehow. The bridge at Nimrod and the canoe landing loomed out of the fog much sooner than expected.

We wandered into the J&J Bar for a quick bite to eat before hitting the road. Shelly found a signal on her smartphone and read from the screen while we waited for burgers. "According to Wikipedia," she said, "Brigadoon is a play—a musical about a Scottish village that appears only once every hundred years. So it's not even a myth—just some old writer's fantasy. Jerry must be Scottish or something."

"Must be," I replied. "I'm going to ask where it's at. Maybe we could stop by and thank him."

I got up and walked over to an old guy sitting at the end of the bar with his Sunday morning tap beer and tomato juice. "Say, we met a guy at a nice house upriver a ways while we were canoeing. His name was Jerry and he called his farm 'Brigadoon.' Can you tell me how to get there?"

The old guy thought for minute or two. I'm sure he would have taken a drag on his cigarette if he still could legally smoke one here.

"Nope," he said. "I've lived here for over sixty years and I've never heard of a 'Brigadoon'." And the only Jerry I know is the bartender over there. What were you smokin' out there on the river?"

I walked back and sat down. Shelly looked at me. "Well, did he give you directions?"

"Aahh, no," I said. "Looks like maybe we have to come back in a hundred years and take another canoe trip if we want to thank Jerry."

Random Acts of Plowing

Nonfiction—Guest Writer

by Jim "Snow" Lein

The need to write seems to run in my family's genes. Both of my sons have been known to try their hand at it and my younger brother Jim pens a monthly column called "Steep Thoughts" for *Colorado Serenity* magazine out in Denver. He left Minnesota many moons ago for the bright shiny lights of the ski slopes of the Colorado mountains and stayed to raise a family. But with skiing and mountains comes snow. You can't escape that. ("Random Acts of Plowing" was previously published in *Colorado Serenity* magazine.)

For many years, I relied on the sun for snow removal. But a shaded, icy bend in my driveway can challenge even the most surefooted vehicle. Presnowplow, each time a storm rolled through, I'd peer out the window, steaming cup of cocoa in hand, and frown with concern as I watched my wife scrape and shovel the curve down to the pavement.

Then a friend offered me a sweet deal on his red Honda ATV with a shiny yellow plow. I hesitated until my wife bopped me on the head with a battle-scarred shovel. Soon after, I awoke one December Saturday morning to a foot of powder blanketing the driveway.

The garage door rattled open. The Honda growled to life and dropped its blade. I had no training—not even *Snowplowing for Dummies.* And plowing dry practice runs in the fall might have made my neighbors wonder if I had finally lost it. So I just mimicked the county plow drivers. *I have a Masters degree. How hard could it be?* On that first pass, bone-dry snow blew past my goggles like face shots you experience skiing Vail on a powder day. The hungry Honda made short work of the driveway. I surveyed the landscape for bigger challenges. Since plowing was so fun, why not randomly knock off a few more driveways? Maybe store up some goodwill for the next time I tick somebody off by leaving my garbage cans out three days after pickup.

My neighbor Paul was chugging along with his temperamental snowblower. I'd snitched firewood from his stack once—maybe twice. I swerved around him, pirouetting in front of the garage, and cleared his driveway in a dozen passes. *Thanks for the firewood. I* made short work of the long and rutted lane of Rolf and Sondra, elderly neighbors. No one was home to witness my labor. *My reward will be in heaven.* Next, I cleared the short, flat driveway of John, an overseas airline pilot. He emerged from the house brandishing a bottle of wine like a waiter at a fine restaurant. "This is my favorite Israeli vintage," he said. I accepted the gift to make John feel good. *Yet another selfless act.* And so on, and so on.

That evening, I lounged before a crackling stack of Paul's pine, sipping a fine Israeli wine—the model man-of-the-house and beloved neighborhood Good Samaritan. I toasted myself, flames shimmering through burgundy-tinted liquid. The phone rang. "Jeem!" Rolf cried in heavily accented English. "Sondra and I are so grateful. She is terrified of being snowed in. She has a condition, you know." *No problem.*

The next weekend a ferocious storm dropped four feet of heavy snow. Whistling merrily, I mounted the ATV—unaware that some hard lessons in plowing lurked outside the door. Lesson One: ATVs cannot push four feet of snow uphill. Six feet from the garage the wheels churned desperately. Paul and his finicky snowblower crept toward my garage, clearing an escape route for my Honda. Coincidentally the route led right up to his garage so of course I cleared his driveway first, one downhill-only, gravity-assisted run after another.

Then my cellphone rang. "Jeem!" Rolf exclaimed. "What is your plan? Sondra has a condition, you know!" I did not have a plan or a clue. Lesson Two: Always push the snow as far off the driveway as possible. Rolf's long rutted driveway was like an icy Winter Olympics luge course. My plow blade bucked off the walls of snow hardened like concrete since my plowing debut. I had to push each load hundreds of feet down

Rolf's driveway and dump it on the main road. Lesson Three: Keep your jacket hood down to avoid becoming the hood ornament of a passing county plow as you plunge blindly onto the road. Lesson Four: Memorize in the offseason any decorative landscaping near the driveways you intend to randomly plow. *Sorry about the lawn gnome, John.*

It snowed hard as darkness fell. I stuffed iPod earbuds under my faux rabbit fur flaps to temper the mind-numbing tedium and laced my cocoa with just a nip of schnapps. I didn't want to get busted for PWI— Plowing While Intoxicated. Carpal-tunnel-like spasms twisted my hand, worn out from hours of shifting between forward and reverse. Falling snow melted on my gaudy hat and trickled down the back of my spine as a precursor to hypothermia. Hours after dark, I limped on fumes down that first solitary path Paul had cut through my own snow-clogged driveway.

Mother Nature delivered four consecutive weekend storms that December. By New Year's Day, my driveway was a miniature relief of the Grand Canyon, towering ramparts of granite-like snow. Unsuspecting visitors, who should have looked first and never entered, plugged their vehicles between the canyon walls as they attempted a belated turnaround.

Legend has it that Eskimos have as many as four hundred words for "snow." I've added a few more colorful adjectives to their vocabulary if they are interested. My strategy now is "Considerate" Acts of Plowing. But I always get to Rolf's driveway, eventually. Sondra has a condition, you know.

64709507R00138

Made in the USA
Lexington, KY
17 June 2017